DISCARD

OWEN COUNTY PUBLIC LIBRARY
10 SOUTH MONTGOMERY ST.
SPENCER, IN 47460

IN DADDY'S SHOES

Other Available Books by Sandra Elzie:

The Diplomatic Tutor

IN DADDY'S SHOES

•

Sandra Elzie

OWEN COUNTY PUBLIC LIBRARY
10 SOUTH MONTGOMERY ST.
SPENCER, IN 47460

AVALON BOOKS
NEW YORK

© Copyright 2010 by Sandra Elzie
All rights reserved.
All the characters in the book are fictitious,
and any resemblance to actual persons,
living or dead, is purely coincidental.
Published by Avalon Books,
an imprint of Thomas Bouregy & Co., Inc.
160 Madison Avenue, New York, NY 10016

Library of Congress Cataloging-in-Publication Data

Elzie, Sandra.
 In daddy's shoes / Sandra Elzie.
   p. cm.
 ISBN 978-0-8034-7785-8
 1. War Widows—Fiction.   2. Teachers—Fiction.   I. Title.
 PS3605.L95I5 2010
 813'.6—dc22
                                                    2010016292

PRINTED IN THE UNITED STATES OF AMERICA
ON ACID-FREE PAPER
BY HADDON CRAFTSMEN, BLOOMSBURG, PENNSYLVANIA

To my daughter, Kim, who has
always believed in me.

Chapter One

Lydia Reynolds pulled into her driveway, punched the remote to open the garage door, and contemplated all that she had dealt with during the day. She refused to think about what she had waiting for her the next week. No wonder she had a shooting pain tightening her neck and creeping up into the back of her head.

She automatically glanced at the clock beside the radio dials, glad to see that she was home ten minutes early. Maybe she'd make hamburgers and french fries and not worry about preparing a big meal. A night off from major cooking would be a great way to start her two-day reprieve from the office. She deserved a break after the nonstop week she had just spent appeasing the demanding attorney she worked for.

For just a moment she slumped in the bucket seat. Her exhaustion brought back memories of the life she and Steven, her late husband, had planned. They were going to have a half dozen children, and she would stay home to raise them until they were all in school. It seemed as if life had handed her the glass slipper, only to shatter those Cinderella dreams into a thousand shards.

Now she was a widow with a fatherless son and a stressful job. No fairy tale there. But despite her life being different than she had expected, she still had a road to travel and a child to shepherd to adulthood. She would make the best of it. Her beloved son was more than worth it.

The garage door was closing behind her little white Ford hybrid as she stepped out and slammed the door, still thinking about dinner. She wasn't even sure she was up to grilling hamburgers. Was there something even easier that she could whip up on a warm, late-September evening? A tiny smile lifted the corners of her mouth as she considered her options. It was Friday; maybe she'd have pizza delivered so she and Brandon could watch a movie and relax together.

Her smile broadened as she thought about the time her ten-year-old son had told her that a Pizza Hut delivery was the best meal she had ever cooked. Not the highest praise for her culinary skills, of course, but what ten-year-old didn't love pizza?

When she entered the kitchen, her eyes were immediately drawn to Brandon's backpack, which was still on the counter where it had been when she put his sack lunch next to it that morning. Had he forgotten his books today? The lunch was missing, so he must have remembered to take that at least.

She hefted the backpack, crossed the living room, and headed into Brandon's bedroom. There she stopped dead in her tracks, and her mouth dropped open. Her reaction jetted past surprise to land with a splash in a pool of confusion and anger. She didn't want to believe what she was seeing—or what it implied.

In Daddy's Shoes

Brandon was sneaking into his bedroom through a window. He straddled the sill, a look of utter shock and guilt in his wide eyes when he heard the door open and looked up to see his mother standing there, framed in the doorway, holding his backpack in front of her like a shield.

Mother and son sucked in their breath simultaneously, mentally adjusting to the situation.

"Uh, hi, Mom," Brandon said, pulling himself on into the room. Once in, he stood up, shifting his weight from one foot to the other, dropping his gaze to avoid looking directly at his mother. His arms hung limply at his sides for a few seconds before he cocked his hip to one side, adjusting his thin, preteen body to a nonchalant stance designed to make her think he was relaxed and innocent. It didn't take long for him to slump a little when he realized his ruse wasn't working. He shifted his weight to his other foot, shoved his hands into his pockets, and stared at the floor as he waited to hear what his mother would say.

Lydia surveyed her son, willing the shock to wear off. Like his father, he had unruly brown hair, which was forever flopping forward into his eyes.

When she had first met Steven Reynolds early on in high school, he had been slender, but by the time he was a junior, he had filled out to be a real threat on the football field, the baseball field, and the wrestling mats. They had nicknamed him Steamroller Reynolds for his ability to "roll over" any opposition.

As she stared at Brandon, silent and unable to look her in the eye, she saw a miniature of her husband. She wasn't sure about such things, but Brandon probably had the potential to be as great an athlete as his father. He would, sooner or later, no doubt, follow in his father's sure, determined footsteps, but lately he was testing every limit and struggling with the anger and frustration he seemed to feel toward everything and everyone. His once-sweet personality was rapidly sliding downhill, and Lydia was at her wit's end on how to deal with him. Not for the first time she wished he had a father to turn to.

Her arms relaxed, dropping the backpack to her side as she took a couple of fortifying breaths before speaking. Brandon looked so much like Steven that she had a difficult time staying angry with him for long. She couldn't look at her son without remembering that he was still grieving the loss of his father to a sniper bullet in Iraq. Two years didn't seem to have mellowed his grief. If anything, it had hardened it into anger.

"Would you care to explain where you've been and what you're doing crawling into the house through a window that was supposed to be locked so burglars can't get in and rob us?" Her voice had not risen, but her overtaxed brain was shooting off fireworks behind her eyes, and the hint of a headache that her mind had been flirting with was now taking over, demanding attention. Why had Brandon started acting out so much lately?

She forced her back to remain straight, her shoulders square, and her head high as she stared down at her son, who had started to pick at a scab on the back of one hand.

Without thinking, she reached out, placing her hand over his to stop his nervous fingers while she waited for him to speak.

"Uh, well, I wanted to go play outside after school, and

In Daddy's Shoes 5

when I went out, the door locked behind me," he said, looking just to the left of her. "Lucky for me, the window was open," he said, although his jerky smile never rose above his lips.

His shrug slammed into her stomach like a fist. He was lying to her. She knew it. But why? She'd raised him to be honest and forthright and to know that he could trust her with anything. The shrug implied that she was making too much out of whatever had happened. It meant that he thought it was "no big deal." Well, she thought, as her temper started a slow climb from barely warm to blast-furnace boil, this was important. Very important.

She took a deep breath before answering. She knew she needed to keep calm . . . even if it killed her.

"That is so obviously a lie, Brandon, that I won't tolerate it. You know what I've taught you about telling the truth. Well, you just had your chance to tell me the truth, and you blew it. You will stay in your room for the entire weekend except to go to the bathroom."

His eyes snapped up to collide with hers as she tossed his backpack to the floor near his desk. He opened his mouth to protest but closed it without uttering a word.

She could tell he was fuming, and though he had been caught red-handed, still he wouldn't back down. Well, it was her responsibility as his parent to make sure that he learned that "crime" didn't pay.

Brandon stubbornly crossed his arms, lowering his chin until his jaw was locked into a pout that silently screamed with anger and resentment.

She shook her head and turned to leave his room, closing the door softly behind her. No more recriminations. He could just sit there and think about telling the truth in the future. Praying he had done nothing dangerous in his sneaking around, she held her breath until she was almost to the kitchen. Then tears slid down her face, leaving a wet trail of disappointment and frustration.

It was in these moments that she cursed the day Steven had told her he wanted to join the Air Force. She had been so proud of him for wanting to do his part to serve the country and keep America free, but he had left her to deal with the sometimes overwhelming situations of parenthood all alone, and now she wished she could go back in time and beg him not to go. It was in these moments that she wanted to relive the conversation when she and her new husband had discussed his desire for a military career— the military career that had led to his death. If she could relive those moments, if she could have known then what she knew now, she would have asked him to reconsider, to think of her and his family.

But she had been pretty young. Would she have given him an ultimatum about choosing the military or her? As she pressed her hands to her temples and gently pushed against her pounding headache, she wasn't even sure which choice Steven would have made. She was sure he had loved her, had loved Brandon, but he had loved his country just as much.

She pushed the useless thoughts from her brain and tried to refocus on what she needed to do now. She had to deal with today, and she had to come up with a strategy to deal with Brandon. She had talked with the guidance counselor at his school, but the aging woman had said mildly that Brandon was making good grades, socializing well, and steering clear of dangerous behaviors like experimenting with alcohol or drugs.

Clearly, Brandon was acting out at home, with her. Did he somehow blame her for not being as good a father as she was a mother? But what could she do about that? She couldn't miraculously produce testosterone or create more hours in a day. But she sensed she needed some assistance in directing him down the path he should be traveling. As things were at home right now, in a few years he'd probably end up in juvenile court.

She had to do something. She couldn't just sit by and watch him self-destruct. Ignoring the situation with the hope that it would get better or that he'd grow out of this phase wasn't the answer.

Lydia opened the cupboard, grabbed the aspirin bottle, and popped it open to shake two pills into her hand. Even as she ran water into a cup and downed the pills in one swallow, her mind was still focused on her erring son.

She didn't enjoy punishing Brandon, but lately it seemed she had to do that more and more often. What was she going to do? Whom could she turn to for help? Her own father had passed away the prior year, and since Steven's father lived a fair distance away—and had Steven's mom to contend with on a daily basis—it left Brandon with no consistent male role model in his life. Maybe that was the answer.

She took an angry swipe at her tears, turning to grab the phone book and flip to the Yellow Pages.

"Where is it? Bibles," she muttered, running a finger down the page. "Big Al's World of Cars . . . ah, here it is, Big Brothers of America." She had heard their advertisements on the radio. Maybe what Brandon needed was to spend time with a man doing the kinds of things that guys did.

She had been excited when he was assigned to Mr. Jenkins' fourth-grade class. She'd heard only good things about the personable, energetic teacher, and she'd hoped that Brandon's having a man instructing him would help his self-confidence. But over the past few weeks since school started, it didn't seem to have made any difference. If anything, Brandon was getting even more rebellious.

Well, she would meet the man herself at the upcoming parent/teacher conference night in just over a week.

She slid the book over the counter toward the phone as she turned her attention to the blinking light that indicated a call she had missed. She punched the button and waited impatiently for the recording to start.

Beep. "Good afternoon, this is Andrew Jenkins, Brandon's teacher." *Speak of the devil!* "I'm sorry I missed you, but I was wondering how Brandon is doing. The office told me he's been out all week with the flu, so I'm calling to see if there's a way to get his homework assignments to him so he can work on them and not get too far behind. If you could call me at home tonight"—he left a number—"I'd appreciate it. I have his assignments and one of his books with me, so maybe we can meet this weekend, and I can give them to you. Thank you."

Lydia stared at a polished brass knob on a cabinet door, transfixed on the sunlight reflecting off the shiny surface. She felt numb as the teacher's words penetrated the shock that was clogging her brain.

Brandon had skipped school—not just today but for five whole days! For five days he had been roaming the streets doing God knows what with God knows whom and no doubt totally oblivious to the dangers out there! *Oh, Lord.* A shudder ran through her at the thought of his being kidnapped or worse. It wasn't just in Iraq that people died. How was she supposed to handle this?

Since Steven had been killed two years earlier, she had dealt with a lot of things that she had never thought about handling alone. She had buried her husband and later her mother and then her father. She even felt like she had buried the safe, fairy-tale life she once knew. Her need to provide for herself and her son had driven her from her comfort zone as a homemaker and into the job market. Now she was juggling a demanding job and trying to be both mother and father to an angry, hurting little boy.

"I can't do this," she whispered, sinking down to her knees on the kitchen tiles, the slim skirt of her navy suit riding up. Her hands covered her face as tears found their way around her fingers, dripping onto her legs. "I can't do this alone anymore."

Feeling incapable of handling the burdens resting squarely on her two stooped shoulders was becoming nearly a daily ritual. Things with Brandon weren't getting better; they were getting worse, much worse. She bowed her head, crying until the well of tears dried up and her head throbbed. She was at the end of her rope with no knot to hang on to. She felt hopeless, without a clue what to do next.

With a swipe at her cheeks with the back of her hand, she reached up to grasp the edge of the cabinet and stand, then turned toward the refrigerator for something cold to drink.

What *could* she do? Her mind whirled as she twisted the cap off a bottle of water before sliding onto one of the bar stools and pressing her aching head against the chilled plastic bottle.

"I have to work, and that means leaving Brandon either with a babysitter or by himself," she mumbled. "It's only for an hour or so after school, but he's so young, and now I can't trust him to stay safe."

She rolled her eyes as she thought about trying a sitter again. Brandon resented being treated like a child and had announced that, since he was in fourth grade, he was old enough to come home and let himself into the house. She had never once considered having a latchkey kid, but there she was.

"Life isn't always easy." She had heard Steven say that more times than she cared to count, but it didn't make this situation any less stressful. *"You can't always have everything you want."* Well, duh. She could testify to the truth in that statement if she was ever called as a witness. "Going back to work so soon was never on my agenda either," she muttered, pressing her fingers against her temples as she straightened her back. "But I did what I had to do back then, and I'll do what I have to do now for Brandon."

Maybe she should have stayed in San Antonio near the Air Force base, where she had had friends. Instead she had buckled under pressure from her parents to move back to Georgia, where she had grown up, so they could help her with Brandon. Had she made a poor choice? Only God knew the answer to that sixty-four-thousand-dollar question.

She frowned as she reached for a tissue to dry her face and blow her nose. It always disturbed her when people

In Daddy's Shoes 11

wallowed in self-pity, and here she was, mucking it up with the best of them.

"Grow up, girl," she told herself as she turned to toss the soiled tissue. She was still berating herself as she hiked up her hopelessly wrinkled skirt and pulled off her panty hose before yanking the skirt back down and padding barefoot through the kitchen.

"Okay, Lydia, what are you going to do about this situation?" She stared at her shadowy reflection in the smoked-glass front of the cabinet that held her crystal wineglasses.

"Maybe I'll open that white Zinfandel. I'm tired of saving it for a special occasion that never happens," she told her reflection before turning around to lean back against the counter to think.

She dropped her head forward, her chin on her chest as she pulled the clip from her hair, allowing it to fall forward around her face, releasing the pressure of the upswept do. Lydia flinched when the phone rang, the headache still lingering.

When it shrilled a second time, she reached over and grabbed the receiver, tucking it against her ear. She closed her eyes and concentrated on relaxing her neck, in hopes of lessening the tension and stalling the migraine that she definitely was not in the mood for.

"Hello?" Her voice squeaked out, surprising her. She cleared her throat and tried again. "Hello?" This time the person on the other end must have understood, since she heard a soft chuckle.

"I'm sorry for laughing," came the disembodied voice over the phone. "This is Andy Jenkins again. I need to speak with Mrs. Reynolds about Brandon," he concluded. After a few moments of silence, he continued. "Is this a bad time? Should I call back later?"

Great, she thought. She was working herself into a full-blown headache capable of splitting her head in two, but first she had to deal with Brandon's teacher. Well, she really wanted to talk with him too, just not tonight. Tonight she wanted the aspirin to take effect and have a relaxing glass of wine. Even though it might not be a good idea to mix aspirin with alcohol, she was beyond caring.

"Um, no, that's okay, Mr. Jenkins. I just got home a few minutes ago and got your message." *And my son just sneaked in his bedroom window after spending the day— the week—doing God knows what.*

"I was just checking on Brandon and wondering if I could drop off his lessons so that maybe you could work with him this weekend to get him caught up. If he's feeling up to it yet, that is."

His voice sounded nice, and he seemed concerned about Brandon, but she wasn't in any shape to talk with anyone right now. The last thing she needed was company.

"I'm only a couple of blocks away, and it won't take but five minutes to drop off his assignments," coaxed the teacher.

He seemed determined, and she didn't have the strength to resist.

"Fine. Come on over." She was sure he heard her lack of enthusiasm, but that was just too bad. She hung up the phone, continuing to stare at the offending object for several seconds before turning to the refrigerator for that bottle of wine.

Chapter Two

Lydia's wineglass was half empty by the time the doorbell rang. She needed to rid herself of her headache and relax so she could tackle working with Brandon and his week's worth of homework. But first she had to deal with the man who was standing on her porch. The man she had hoped to meet the next week.

She peeked through the window, and there was Brandon's teacher. She took in the dark brown hair, absently, noting that he must use mousse to get it to stick out all over the top in that very fashionable and attractive style. Steven had never had hair long enough to mousse.

Dark eyes stared straight ahead, and his face was clean-shaven, even though he had a five o'clock shadow that gave him a Don Johnson appearance.

"He looks harmless enough," she whispered to herself as she stepped back from the door.

She had to admit that, even though she hadn't been able to see much, at least his face was pleasant, and he obviously cared enough about Brandon to put in this personal appearance.

With the door already swinging open, she remembered she had been crying, must look a wreck, and was standing there with a glass of wine in her hand. What a great first impression. The teacher would probably think she was an unfit mother.

"Hi. I'm Lydia Reynolds." She continued to hold the door only partially open. Should she invite him in?

"Hello, Mrs. Reynolds. I'm Andy Jenkins." When she just stared at him as if in a trance, he continued. "May I come in and go over these assignments with you?" He held a book up for her to see.

She stepped back even as her hand fluttered up to brush loose hairs away from her face. "Oh, certainly," she said in a rush. "And please call me Lydia."

He couldn't help but notice that Brandon's mother was attractive . . . and had been crying. Casting common sense aside, he brushed past her, close enough to catch a faint, sweet fragrance. Perfume? Deodorant? Whatever. It suited her.

Once inside, he turned, allowing his eyes to make a quick perusal down her back to her bare feet before snapping back to her disheveled shoulder-length hair the color of warm honey.

She turned from closing the door. "Um, would you care for a drink? I have wine, sparkling water, or cola," she offered. Her voice was soft and feminine, but it didn't seem to be on purpose. No, he didn't think she was a games-player like his ex-wife, Sheryl. This woman was soft and fragile. And she had been crying.

In Daddy's Shoes

He could tell that he was making her nervous and that she would rather he not be there, but a sick student was more important than his mom's uncomfortable feelings. Besides, he only needed a couple of minutes to explain the assignments.

The manners he had learned as a child told him to bow out quickly and leave the woman alone, but he had never been particularly good at following rules. And right now he wanted to stay and get to know Lydia Reynolds a little better. Maybe that would give him the key to young Brandon Reynolds' barely concealed anger at the world.

Brandon reminded him of himself many years before, after his father had been killed by a drunk driver, leaving his mother with two children to raise. At twelve years old he had felt responsible for the little family and had tried to be good for his mother, but soon he was frustrated, angry, and making everyone around him miserable. He had heard about Brandon's father, and he understood what the boy was going through, without having a dad to help him handle growing up.

"I'd love a cola, if it's not too much trouble." His mother was probably turning over in her grave, vowing to come back and haunt him for blatantly ignoring the rules of etiquette she had tried so hard to teach her two children. *Sorry, Mom.*

Lydia Reynolds' slight frown didn't escape his notice, but he was beyond caring at the moment. It was Friday night, he had an hour before he was to meet the guys for pool, and he had nothing else to do. He might as well spend a few minutes here and try to get to know this woman a little bit. She was possibly five and a half feet tall, but her slender figure gave her the appearance of being small.

After a moment's hesitation, she turned, set her wineglass on the coffee table, and headed for the kitchen. "Take a seat and make yourself comfortable. I'll be right back," she tossed over her shoulder as she disappeared into the kitchen.

Comfortable? How could he relax when he was in the room with a beautiful woman who had fuchsia nail polish on her toes and was obviously upset? Her eyes were red and slightly swollen, and if he was in his right mind, he would be running the other way as fast as his legs could carry him. At least this woman hadn't been crying to jerk his chain, to make him do things he didn't want to do, as Sheryl had done in years past. No, a crying female might always make him uncomfortable, but tears no longer had power over him. He had learned his lesson, and he wasn't going to get caught in that kind of web again. He was here to deliver Brandon's homework assignments and that was all. Period. End of story.

"Okay, idiot," he muttered to himself, "if you're so smart and don't like being around crying women, why in heaven's name are you here when this woman is upset and apparently doesn't want you here?" He didn't have an immediate answer, but he knew he couldn't walk out the door and leave her to drink wine and cry alone.

He wondered how much she had drunk so far. She carried herself too well to have consumed much. Well, he'd drink the soda, give her the assignments, encourage her to work with Brandon to get them done over the weekend so the boy didn't fall too far behind, and then he'd be gone. He had a date with a cue stick.

He sat on the sofa nearest the chair where she had set

In Daddy's Shoes 17

the wineglass and tried to relax. Later he would figure out why he hadn't just handed her the book and left.

In the kitchen, Lydia busied herself getting down a cobalt blue water glass and pushing it against the ice cube button on the front of the refrigerator door. Then she slowly filled the glass and paused for a moment before returning to the living room.

She liked Andy Jenkins' smile, but he was a little overwhelming. He easily stood a foot over her five feet five, and he had broad shoulders. Boy, would she love to be able to just lean on someone like him for a while, let someone else take care of her problems.

A sigh puffed out as she picked up the glass and turned around. "Good-looking men think women should fall at their feet," she muttered with disgust as she headed back toward the living room.

As she made her way past Brandon's skateboard leaning against a wall, she couldn't help comparing the man in her living room with the man she had married. After starting to date Steven in high school, she had never looked seriously at another man. Then, when he had been killed in Iraq, she had been too wrapped up in her grief and that of her son to notice anyone who might have tried to get her attention. Not that Mr. Jenkins was trying to get her attention. But he was the first male, other than family, to sit in her living room in two years. It made her feel strange, as if she was committing a sin, being unfaithful. *Nonsense.* This was Brandon's teacher, and he was here about her son and his assignments. There was nothing for her to worry about.

She paused just outside the living room door, stood a little straighter, and sucked in and blew out a cleansing breath to clear her mind. Mentally fortified, she pushed the swinging door with one elbow.

"I hope diet is all right, since that's all I have." She smiled as she set the glass on a coaster in front of him.

"That's fine. We all get too much sugar in our diets as it is." He smiled too as he picked up the glass and held it high as if toasting her.

"So," she said, sitting down and trying to relax while her brain was pounding an SOS rhythm in her skull. The aspirin wasn't working. "Oh, excuse me for just a moment."

He watched with interest as she glided back to the kitchen. The connecting door remained open. He watched as she reached up into the cupboard, pulling out a small white bottle. When she turned, he quickly averted his eyes, looking toward the fireplace mantel, where several framed pictures were sitting. Once she sat down, put a couple of white pills into her mouth, and chased them with a swallow of wine, he realized it was pain he was seeing in her eyes.

"I'm sorry. I didn't realize you weren't feeling well. Let me just leave this book and the list of assignments," he said, indicating the textbook he had set on the coffee table in front of him. "The sheet explains the assignments. The rest of the books he'll need must already be here at home."

He stood, motioning toward the book. "I've written my name and number on the assignment sheet, so if you have any questions, you can give me a call." He turned to head for the door.

Lydia could hardly believe her luck. Most males wouldn't have put two and two together to realize she didn't feel well,

In Daddy's Shoes

and even if they had, they might not have left so readily. So at least he was polite, even if he was persistent.

She frowned slightly as she realized that, even though Mr. Jenkins was heading toward the door, she wasn't sure that was still what she wanted. Maybe he could help her understand what was going on with Brandon lately.

"Wait a minute, please," she said, jumping up and taking a couple of steps toward him, one hand outstretched as if to grab his arm but stopping just short of touching him.

"Please," she said softly.

He stopped and looked over his shoulder, straining to hear what she had said even as he told himself not to listen but to get out while he could.

"I would really like for you to stay. I'd like to ask you a couple of questions, if that's all right."

The blush that invaded her neck and face was charming, gluing his feet to the hardwood floor and effectively preventing him from leaving, even though he wanted to. Well, actually, he had wanted to leave a few minutes ago, but for some reason he was having different thoughts now. There was something about this woman....

"Come on, sit down." She motioned toward the sofa. "I'd really like to pick your brain about Brandon. He's been . . . acting out a lot lately, and I'm . . . worried about him," she admitted—reluctantly, it seemed. When he didn't move, instead continuing to stare at her, she ventured, "That's really why you're here, right?"

What could he say? Of course that was why he was there. The boy was bright and personable, yet lately he had started to brood and fall behind a little. And now, after missing school for a week, he could be in real trouble.

"Yes, I thought we should touch base," he said, running a hand down the thigh of his jeans to dry his suddenly damp palm.

He watched her tongue slip out to nervously moisten her lips, and his heart rate suddenly increased despite his attempts to keep his mind on the matter at hand. He saw her swipe at a tear.

He cleared his throat. "When I checked in the office for your number and address, I was told that you are a . . . widow. A single mother. I'm sorry for your loss." He didn't tell her that that knowledge was part of what had compelled him to come. He'd figured that being a fatherless preteen might be part of the problem with Brandon.

"You know, a lot of boys in single-parent homes start to rebel just before reaching their teen years. Sometimes they grow out of it, but I don't think it's wise to ignore erratic behavior and just hope it goes away," he said, shoving his fingers into the front pockets of his jeans. He was uneasy about appearing to pry or offer unwanted advice. Single parents had a tough row to hoe, and he didn't want Brandon's mom to feel criticized or attacked.

She was watching him as if she was waiting for him to continue, and it was making him nervous. He lifted one hand to ram his fingers into his hair. He was a virtual stranger, for goodness sake. Would he be able to help? Did he even want to get involved? Yes. His mother had needed help with him, and it was only right to pay it forward.

"What did you have in mind? How do you think I can help?"

"Well, maybe I could tell you about his home life?" she started. "See what you think?"

In Daddy's Shoes

He felt her discomfort. He could tell that she was having a difficult time. He bet she never asked anyone for help. Too independent? Too proud? Too alone? He could tell by the deep breath that slowly seeped out of her that she was nervous and trying to give herself time to collect her thoughts and organize what she wanted to say.

"I'm a little uncomfortable sharing about Brandon's life, because it means telling you about mine," she said quietly. Her gaze dropped as she clenched her hands together to still their trembling.

He wasn't sure he wanted to hear about this woman's late husband, their son, and their life together. He wasn't sure he wanted to know how or why the faceless man had died or how her and her son's lives had been since his passing. Did he want to take on someone else's troubles, offer suggestions on how to improve their lives, when he wasn't even able to figure out how to improve his own? Who was he kidding? He couldn't do her any good. He might as well leave.

"Please, sit down," she coaxed, concentrating on picking up her wineglass to allow him the privacy and time to make up his mind.

Even as his feet moved to take him back into her living room, he could feel a noose tightening around his neck. It was like the movie of his life was rerunning. This woman needed his help, but would he be able to help her?

Chapter Three

Their conversation was stilted at first, both suddenly awkward. Finally Lydia took the reins.

"I guess I'll start," she began, an embarassed smile touching her mouth and disappearing in the next instant, like a hummingbird flitting on to another flower after a quick drink. She wrapped both hands around her wineglass. She no longer wanted the wine, but it gave her something to do while her mind scrambled to find a good place to start.

"Steven, Brandon's father, joined the Air Force right after college, and we moved around every couple of years. Brandon was born in Mississippi while his father was in flight school, and then we spent most of our time in San Antonio, Texas, where Steven was a pilot trainer." She took a deep breath and focused her mind backward in time. There had been some rough times, but she had loved Steven, and there had been some very good times as well.

"In the beginning we were very happy, at least as a family, but I didn't realize that Steven wanted more out of life, wanted more out of his military career." She nervously

In Daddy's Shoes

drew her eyes back to Andy. "I guess it wasn't enough to go up in a jet and then let some brand-new trainee take the controls and try to execute the maneuver for the day. I think Steven wanted more."

Andy didn't say anything, just watched her glance down at her hands clenching the glass and waited for her to continue. He was uncomfortable, but he felt compelled to know the whole story.

"Anyway," she finally whispered, clearing her throat and raising her voice before continuing, "he came home one night and told me that he had put in for a transfer, volunteering to go to Iraq to fly sorties over the desert." She took a deep breath at the end that she allowed to whoosh out slowly as she leaned back into the leather sofa. She looked like a balloon that had lost all of its air. Deflated.

"How long was he in Iraq?" Andy wasn't sure why he had asked about the guy, but he was drawn to the story and had to hear the ending. He was having a hard time understanding a man who would get tired of being with a beautiful wife and a great little boy, but he was glad there were men willing to serve, willing to go, willing to give their lives for their country. Still, if it had been his choice, he was sure he would have stayed home with his wife and son.

"He was there less than a year when his plane was shot down. In fact"—she smiled slightly—"the irony is that he was scheduled to come home in a little over two weeks."

She could see the look in Andy's eyes. She had seen it before. She had learned to read the pity in the eyes of people who heard about the death of her husband.

"I know Steven loved his country," she continued, "more than anyone or anything else, and even though he was helping his country by training pilots, his personality drove him to want to be on the front lines. I try to console myself that he was following his dream, but when I look at our son, who needs his father, it's difficult not to be angry at how things turned out," she admitted softly.

"I came to terms with Steven's personality many years ago, and although there were days when I almost hated him for what I saw as reckless selfishness when he raced his motorcycle or flew jets, I was also proud that he had been willing to give up his easy, safe job on American soil and put his life on the line for the country he loved. Then . . . then he was killed."

She stopped talking for a moment, took a deep breath, and held it for a few seconds.

"After his death it took me a long time to get past the bitterness. But, as time passed, I had more proud days than angry ones. Of course there are days when I wonder what life would have been like if he hadn't died. Who knows what would have happened? But our life is nothing like what Steven and I planned. No part of our life has been easy or carefree since the death of my husband."

She didn't share with Andy how she had been forced to learn a bit of mental toughness. That toughness usually carried her through the day but often crumbled when the lights were out. She didn't tell him how she saved her tears and self-pity for the nighttime, when she lay alone in her king-sized bed missing the man who had been a loving husband and a terrific father. This session was about Brandon, not her.

"How long ago did he die?" His question interrupted her thoughts, drawing her back to the present to focus on the man sitting in her living room.

In Daddy's Shoes

"Almost two years ago. I thought Brandon was sad but fine. I thought he was missing his father less and less as time went on and focusing more on being proud of the job his father had done and what his father had sacrificed for. I didn't realize he had gone so far astray until just today—when I got home and caught him sneaking in through his bedroom window and then got your message that'd he'd cut school all week!"

The wine sloshed as her hand shot out to set the glass on the coffee table. She bolted up to pace, stopping behind the recliner to stare at Andy, her eyes pleading for him to understand why she was so upset. "His backpack was right where I had set it this morning, but the lunch was gone. At first I thought he had gone to school and forgotten his books. I don't know how I could have been so blind and stupid!" she muttered in self-disgust, her lips firming into a straight line as she turned her back on him.

"Anyway, all that aside," she said, turning back and flinging one hand in irritation, "I'm sure I've been a big part of the problem. I uprooted Brandon from all that was familiar, his friends in school and church, and brought him here to Georgia so I could live near my parents. They had encouraged me to move home, and I guess I was being a little selfish, not thinking of Brandon's losses, only my own, and figuring I could cope better back with family and friends." She shrugged and spread her hands out in front of her, palms up. "I think I blew it," she said softly, her eyes tearing up again.

"Well, I'm no psychologist, but what's done is done, and there's nothing you can do about that now. You can only move forward, right?" When she slowly nodded, he continued. "The way I see it, Brandon's probably angry at the world and everyone in it, and, quite frankly, I'm surprised it's taken him almost two years to start showing it," he said reassuringly.

"The bottom line is that I'm not sure what to do or how to help him." She raised glistening eyes to him. "Before I heard your message about Brandon being absent from school all this week, I was going along blissfully in my own little world, assuming my son was doing all right, when he was really floundering, and I was too busy to notice!"

She closed her eyes for a moment before being able to control her voice. "I was looking up the number for the Big Brothers organization right before I played your message. Do you know if they're any good?" She returned to her seat on the sofa, her fingers trembling slightly as she lowered her eyes for a moment, a silent prayer jetting through her mind as she waited to hear what this man in her son's life would think.

There was a pause before he answered. She opened her eyes to see him staring at her, a slight frown marring his otherwise tanned good looks.

"I don't know too much about the local organization, but the concept is certainly a good one. There are also after-school activities, such as football, track, and swim team, that might interest Brandon. Joining a team sport would keep him busy, give him a chance to do things with other boys his age, and give him a male mentor in the form of a coach."

He watched her whole face transform as hope lit her eyes. She stared at him as if he were a savior come to earth in the flesh. He couldn't believe what it did to his ego to

In Daddy's Shoes

see her smiling at him as if he could fix the world for her. He had heard so many negatives in his life, both while growing up and while married to Sheryl.

"Is it too late for him to join a team?"

"Well, first, you find out if he's even interested in playing football or swimming or any other sport, for that matter. Has he shown an interest before?"

"He used to play softball, and he and his father occasionally threw around a football. He loves the water, but he's not a very good swimmer. He'd need lessons," she concluded.

"Well, why don't you start by asking him if he'd like to participate in one of the sports programs? If he's interested, then he'd *have* to come to school in order to come to practice, and he'd *have* to do his homework, or he wouldn't be allowed to play. Team rules," he added, smiling.

She couldn't believe how quickly Andy Jenkins had come up with a possible solution. Steven had always been athletic, so maybe Brandon would follow in his father's footsteps.

"Would you mind talking with him? It might sound better to him coming from a man and not his mom. Besides, I think I'm the archenemy right now."

Every muscle in Andy's body tightened at her question. Offering a suggestion was one thing, but getting personally involved was another. Hadn't he learned his lesson about getting involved with beautiful and seemingly fragile women?

"No," he said, shaking his head, his eyes never leaving hers. "I think it would be a good idea for Brandon to join a team, but I think the suggestion should come from you. I try not to interfere where there's a parent who is concerned and involved with the child."

"Is that why you're here with Brandon's homework?" She watched his eyes as he stared at her. He was silent, but she wondered if he'd respond to the challenge she had lobbed to his side of the court.

"I don't want . . . I just think his parent should be the one to encourage him. I'll stand behind you, but I don't want to take your place."

The direct simplicity of his words wiped her feet out from under her. She nodded. "Okay. You're right, of course."

"Listen, I brought his work by because I was concerned about his getting behind, but I think the rest is up to you." When she didn't respond, he offered, "Uh, I occasionally do a little after-school tutoring, if he needs it."

"No, he doesn't need a tutor," she sighed, closing her eyes and taking a deep breath before forcing her shoulders to relax. "He's smart," she said, emphasizing her statement by leaning forward. "What he needs is time and attention," admitted. "Some man's time and attention. He needs the kinds of things that a mother can't give him."

"He doesn't need me," he answered, his tone direct, almost fierce. "He has a parent who cares about him."

"Clearly I'm not enough," she said in frustration. "I'm a woman. He doesn't think I understand what he's going through," she hurled at the teacher, turning to grab the glasses from the coffee table before heading for the kitchen.

Andy didn't know what else to say. He could certainly understand her frustration, but he had gotten involved up to his eyebrows the last time, and Sheryl had taken her son, Thomas, with her when she divorced him.

"I care about Brandon," he called out to her, already halfway to the door. "I brought his homework assignments, but I didn't come to *get* a homework assignment. Can you understand that?" He ran a hand through his hair in frustration, walking a couple of steps toward the kitchen before stopping and shoving his hands into the pockets of his jeans.

He stood, waiting for her to storm back out of the kitchen and launch another attack. When she didn't appear, he scrubbed his face with one hand. How had he gotten into the middle of this?

"What am I doing here arguing with the woman?" he asked, his voice just above a whisper. "She wants more than I can give." He continued to stand there, muscles taut, a frown etched on his face. He wanted to give more; he wanted to be able to help the woman with her son, but he couldn't right now. His own wounds were still too new, still too raw. His insides were bleeding, his heart still hurting from the beating it had recently taken.

He looked up to see Lydia Reynolds standing in the doorway to the kitchen. Her shoulders were slightly slumped, but her head was held high, and her eyes bore into his with military precision. At that moment he thought she was the most courageous and beautiful woman he had ever seen. Under different circumstances he would definitely want to get to know her better. But he didn't want to rush into anything. He needed to take his time and not make any more mistakes when it came to women. The only problem was, he knew that Lydia Reynolds didn't have time to wait. Brandon needed help now.

"Lydia, please check out the Big Brother program for

Brandon and also ask him if he'd like to get involved in sports. If he does, and if you run into any problems getting him onto a team now that the year has already started, just give me a call. I'll make sure he gets in."

When she remained silent, just staring at him with eyes that had lost hope again, he silently groaned. He felt like the batter on a losing team, in the bottom of the ninth, two outs, and him with two strikes.

Chapter Four

Brandon crept back to his room, slipped in, and quietly shut the door. He wasn't sure how he felt about Mr. Jenkins coming to his house and talking with his mother, but he knew he wasn't happy about all the homework he would have to do over the weekend. It wasn't fair. He had been sick. Well, not exactly sick, more like "sick" of school. But now his mother knew he had been cutting class all week. Mr. Jenkins had ratted him out and told his mom everything. He was doomed.

He flopped back onto his bed, wondering what his pal Toby was doing. They had planned on going to the movies on Saturday. "Well," he said, clenching his fingers into a fist and slamming it down on the mattress, "that's not happening now." He sighed.

"It's not fair. When Mom calls in sick to work, she doesn't have to do the work the next day. She doesn't get into trouble," he mumbled, jerking his pillow over to stuff under his head as he stared at the ceiling.

It was weird hearing his mom talk with Mr. Jenkins about

his father and how the two of them had played ball together and how she had said he didn't need her but needed a man in his life. He didn't think he needed a man around. Well, not unless it was his father, but that couldn't happen. He wasn't sure if he wanted some man telling him what to do. He'd have to think about that later.

"But it sure was cool when she said I was intelligent." He snickered. The smile hung around as he basked in the glow of such a comment coming from his mom, who was always after him to do this and do that, as if he was stupid or something. "Pretty cool," he mumbled, launching from the bed to grab his softball glove and ball off the bookshelf.

It had been a long time since he had used it. Probably almost two years. He had played with his father, with his friends back in San Antonio, and then with Gramps before he went to heaven too. Did he want to play sports at school? Hmm. "Yeah," he said, tossing the ball into the air and catching it in the mitt with a resounding slap. "It might be cool to play ball again, but only if I can be the pitcher," he murmured, throwing the ball into the glove with more force.

When a light tap sounded on his door, he quickly tossed the ball and glove onto the shelf and flopped onto the bed before answering.

"Yeah?"

"May I come in?"

"Sure, I guess," he called out.

By the time the door opened and his mother stepped inside, he had propped two pillows behind him and had one of his Hot Wheels cars in his hands, fiddling with the tires.

"I think we need to talk about why you stayed out of school for a week." She walked to his bed and sat down, running her hand across his forehead to push his longish hair out of his eyes. He frowned and moved his head a few inches away from her touch.

Her heart was bleeding, but she forced herself to continue. "I'm not sure where to start this discussion, but I guess the first thing I need to know is, what made you stay home from school without permission?" When he said nothing, she frowned. "Of course, I'm assuming that you stayed at home, but you were sneaking in through your window, so I guess you spent the week . . . out and about somewhere?" She waved her arm in an arch, indicating any direction outside the house.

"Nah, I was home almost all the time. I snuck out to see Toby once, but mostly I just watched TV. It got boring after a while," he mumbled, turning his Hot Wheels over and over in his hands.

"But why?"

"I don't like school, I don't like homework, and I don't like Mr. Jenkins. I already told you that a hundred times," he blurted out. "Ah, forget it. You just don't understand," he said, disgust written on his face as he turned his attention back to the car in his hand.

"Maybe I understand, and maybe I don't, but there's no excuse for staying home from school and lying to them . . . or to me. So, over the rest of this weekend, you'll learn to love doing homework, because you'll be doing a lot of it. And as to not liking school, well"—she shrugged—"you'll just have to suck it up and make the best of it, since it's the law that you go. Understand?" She reached over to put her hand on his upper arm, but he jerked away from her touch and slid off the bed to stand looking out the window.

"I'm going to make dinner now, and later we'll talk some more and get started on your homework." When he kept his back to her and didn't answer, she raised her voice. "Understand?"

"Yes! Would you get off it?" His head was down, and his voice had taken on an edge that she hadn't heard before.

It seemed like only a few years ago that he had been a tiny, red-faced, wrinkled newborn, totally dependent upon his parents for everything. Now he was ten years old and pushing the limits to be his own boss, making his own decisions.

It was going to be a very long weekend.

The homework was finally finished, and Brandon was in his room sulking, but Lydia was beyond caring. He had spent all of Saturday and most of Sunday morning complaining about the work she was forcing him to complete and griping that he had the only slave-driving mother in town. It was a good thing he had finished the work, since she was about at the end of her patience.

The weekend had been the longest of her life, but now she was stretched out in the recliner with her eyes closed against the brilliant sun beaming through the window. She had just drifted off to sleep when the phone rudely jolted her awake.

She grabbed it on the second ring, hoping she could get off the phone in a hurry. A headache lurked just behind her eyes, and her back ached from sitting long hours at Brandon's elbow as she prodded him to stay focused on his work.

"Hello?"

In Daddy's Shoes 35

"Hey, girl. Missed you at church today. Is everything okay?"

"Oh, hi, Mary." She headed toward the kitchen for a cool drink. This probably wouldn't be a short conversation. "Everything's fine. I just had some things to take care of."

"You sure everything's all right? You sound sick. Are you coming down with something?"

"No, nothing like that," she said while grabbing a can of Coke from the refrigerator. "I had some trouble with Brandon this past week and we had to spend the weekend taking care of it."

"Is it okay now? Do you need anything?"

"No, we're fine. He cut school last week, and we had to spend the weekend doing a week's worth of homework. At least it's done now, and hopefully he's learned that crime doesn't pay."

"Did he say why he skipped?"

"Not really," she sighed. "Just the usual garbage about hating school, his teacher, et cetera." She sighed again, taking a long swallow of the soda.

"Oh." Mary laughed. "I've heard that one before. Just hang in there, kid, and one of these days he'll be eighteen and out on his own."

"You think so? I was thinking of calling the Big Brothers to see if I can get him a mentor."

"Good idea, but Tammy told me there's almost a year's waiting list. She was checking it out for her boy."

"Really?"

"That's what she said. I guess you'll have to come up with another bright idea. Personally, I think you should get to know Brandon's teacher. He's worth a second look, and I hear he's single. You should check him out," she teased, her voice relaying the smile that must have been on her face.

"Don't even go there," she said, frowning as she toed off her tennis shoes. "I don't have enough time for myself, let alone adding a guy to the mix." She paused, thinking about Andy Jenkins. "Then again, you might have an idea there," she mused aloud.

"What?"

"Well, it just occurred to me that maybe I could persuade the man to give Brandon a little extra attention," she said, smiling to herself.

"What are you planning? What are you up to? Come on," Mary ordered, "tell all."

"I need to think about it and get a plan together. If it works, I'll tell you all about it," she promised, laughing.

"And if it doesn't work?"

"Then I won't want to spread around how I made a fool out of myself. I'll talk to you in a few days," she said, hanging up without waiting for her friend to ask any more questions.

Andy opened his desk drawer, only to shove it closed with one foot. It had been a very long weekend and an even longer Monday.

All weekend he had pondered some of the things Lydia Reynolds had said to him, and his emotional reaction to her words had gone from agreement to anger to frustration. Why him? Why had she homed in on him? Why didn't she pick on one of her male relatives or someone in her church or the guy next door?

He had arrived at school early that morning, setting his

In Daddy's Shoes

coffee on his desk and then letting it grow cold as he stared out the window and thought about deep blue eyes and honey-gold hair that swirled around a face that should be used as a model for paintings. He had even dreamed about her, for goodness sake, but in his dream they hadn't been fighting. Far from it. Damn. He didn't need this distraction. The school year was just getting going.

Brandon had arrived on time to class and had even turned in his homework for the prior week, but he had been sullen, almost angry, when he was called on to answer a question. The boy had slumped in his seat and doodled all day without engaging. Even though he knew that the rules of the class were that he had to make an attempt to answer a question if called upon, the boy had shrugged and mumbled that he didn't know.

He had half expected Brandon's mother to show up with her son that morning and try to start round two of the debate about his helping Brandon, but she hadn't. Thank goodness, although he had caught himself glancing out the window to see if he could spot her car, and at the end of the day he had glanced out several times to see if hers was one of the cars in line to pick up children.

He wasn't sure if he was happy or irritated that she would give up so easily after being so persistent a couple of days ago. Well, he had told her he didn't want to get involved, and he guessed she had gotten the message.

The irritating part was that she had invaded his entire conscious and unconscious life over the weekend. What did it say for a guy to find himself in the middle of watching a football game, his favorite sport, and not know the score or even who had the ball when the game resumed after a Budweiser commercial? "Jeez," he forced through clenched teeth.

"Why did I take the blasted homework over there?" He was still muttering to himself when he stood to leave. He had just stepped around the end of his desk when he stopped in his tracks, his head jerking up at the sound of a soft voice saying his name.

"Mr. Jenkins?"

Man, oh, man, he was in big trouble. In front of him stood Lydia Reynolds in a red and white dress, one hand casually propped on her hip where the dress narrowed to her tiny waist before flaring to a skirt that stopped an inch above her knees. Her honey-blond hair hung down around her shoulders, and she had a smile on her face that would stop a charging bull.

"Oh, good afternoon. How are you?" He licked his suddenly dry lips, standing tall but unsure what step to take next. It was late; he hadn't expected her to show up now.

"I'm fine," she smiled, her big smile adding sparkle to her eyes as she stepped into the room, coming forward with her hand outstretched. "First," she said, her eyes glancing off to the right before she jerked them back to connect with his, "I want to apologize for the way I acted last Friday. I had a splitting headache, and Brandon's escapades were brand-new to me. I was . . . not at my best."

The moment her hand touched his, Andy felt a sizzle. It was as if steam were rising from their clasped hands. He was sure she held on longer than etiquette would say was proper, and his throat was suddenly as dry as the Sahara and stopping all words at the lump of his Adam's apple.

Maybe it was just as well, he reasoned silently. He wasn't

In Daddy's Shoes

sure he could have put together a coherent sentence anyway. He felt trapped, as if she had spun an enticing web and he had stepped right into it. Once he had focused on her red lips, the rest of his world had fallen away, leaving him flailing in that delicious web, unable to move, unable to speak as his eyes followed her every move.

Despite the tear-swollen eyes on Friday night, she had been attractive when he first met her, but now she was stunning. His eyes took a slow cruise from the blond hair tumbling onto her shoulders, down to her feet, and back up, stopping for an extra moment to note the small diamond-studded heart on a thin chain that rested against her tanned skin. A sprinkle of light brown freckles dusted her chest just above the scooped neck of the dress.

He knew he must look like an idiot as he stared at her, open-mouthed, like a baby bird waiting to be fed. At least he *felt* like an idiot. His brain was screaming at him to say something, but he was mesmerized. In mere seconds she had scrambled his brain, leaving him unable to speak. His throat was parched, and his muscles were weak. His hands hung limp at his sides. She slowly turned and started a perusal of the room, stopping every few feet to gaze up at a bulletin board with apparent interest before moving to the next one.

It irritated him that his breathing had deepened and his heart rate had spiked. He couldn't take his eyes off the slender profile of a woman he had met only once but whom he was having trouble getting out of his thoughts.

"I guess I was in shock and took it out on you." She paused to look over her shoulder at him before continuing. "Please forgive me. Actually . . ." she said, turning to face him, her arms relaxing as she slowly slid her hands into pockets hidden in the folds of the cotton dress.

"Actually," she repeated, "I had two reasons for stopping by. One reason," she said, finally reaching his desk, "of course, was to apologize for my behavior. I'm sorry my emotions got away from me." Her gaze dropped for a moment before she dragged her eyes back to meet his and continued. "And the other reason is to see if you've had a chance to think about maybe helping Brandon in whatever ways you *can* manage. Maybe with one of the sports teams you mentioned?"

He knew, even as he tried to control his breathing, which was now coming in shallow spurts, that she knew she had his attention and was using that advantage to attempt to persuade him to be some kind of mentor to her boy. He also knew she was succeeding. He felt a fleeting moment of irritation that he wasn't stronger in the face of temptation, that he was going to give in and do something he probably shouldn't do. He was going to commit precious hours to helping a boy who probably didn't even want his help, and all because he had allowed this slip of a woman and her angry, fatherless son to get under his skin.

He had to admit that it wasn't all her fault. She had simply made him remember why he had become an elementary-school teacher to begin with. To help kids.

Still, he stood mesmerized, his eyes locked with hers, his focus narrowing until she was the only thing in the room. It was just the two of them. She was the breathtaking spider, and he was the fly.

Chapter Five

Lydia hardly remembered leaving the school. Every move, every word, every look Andy Jenkins had given her was imprinted on her mind.

"I can't believe I did that," she muttered for the tenth time as she slowed her car to a stop at a red light. When the idea of seduction had first danced across her mind, it had seemed like a bizarre, unprecedented brainstorm. But now that she had done it, she couldn't decide if she was thoroughly embarrassed or just thrilled that it had seemed to work.

When she turned to look at the car stopped to her left, she realized that a man in the passenger seat was smiling as broadly as she was. She wondered what was making *him* so happy. She returned her attention to the road and her driving, but immediately her mind took her back to Andy Jenkins' classroom and to the man who was going to help Brandon, the man who had agreed to help her son not only with schoolwork but also with after-school activities. She had risked making a gigantic fool of herself, but it had paid off.

She reran the memory like a movie in her mind. When she had asked Andy if he would help Brandon, she saw a change in his facial expression, but she wasn't sure what it meant. His eyes went from focused and stern to relaxed and somewhat glassy, while his stiff posture still signaled loud and clear that he was not comfortable about the situation. But she had been desperate.

"Mr. Jenkins, I know it's none of my business, and please don't hesitate to tell me if you'd rather not answer my question, but I'm wondering," she'd said, turning to face him, leaning back against a bulletin board covered with kids' papers about presidents. "Why did you become a teacher?"

He had moved to the front of his desk, shoving his hands into the pockets of his slacks and relaxing his stance to put most of his weight on his left leg.

He heaved a sigh and glanced down at the floor before answering. "My father taught sixth grade, and I thought he was the smartest man I knew," he acknowledged, raising his eyes to stare at her. "He died when I was young, and my mother didn't remarry. Without any uncles or grandfathers, I had to learn a lot of things on my own. I'm not sure exactly when I decided to follow in my dad's footsteps, but I know I like to teach kids new things, and I love it when they get excited about learning."

She felt like a lawyer who had just asked a question that put the witness on the spot, but she had to admit that his admission surprised her. She concentrated, forcing herself to maintain eye contact, refusing to be the first to look away. Her heart pounded as she waited for him to continue. He glanced toward the door, then at the clock.

She seemed to be making him nervous. But when his

eyes reconnected with hers, *her* stomach lurched. He seemed to be staring not just into her eyes but also through them, to her heart. She was unable to stop the shiver that ran down her spine or the tingle in her toes when the unexplainable sensation reached her feet.

The shiver seemed to awaken her consciousness, her sense of right and wrong. What was she doing? What must he be thinking of her? She had dolled herself up to get his attention, and now that she had it, she wasn't sure what to do next.

She had never been pushy before, yet here she was, trying to push this man into helping her son. She hated to admit how little she knew about dealing with men. She had been with one man in her life, and that man had been her husband. Well, she had started this little play, and she was too old to start crying and run offstage into Mommy's arms. For better or worse, she had to move forward. If begging would help, she'd beg this caring, engaged teacher to work with her son. After all, he would see Brandon every day and could have a profound influence on him, now and in the future.

She remembered that her mother, a pampered but strong woman, had always cautioned her not to be a doormat. She constantly told Lydia to stand up for what she thought was right and to be willing to fight for the things she thought were important. She still missed her mother, who had been very wise. Right now Lydia couldn't think of anything in the world that was more important to her than her son.

She had to admit that she might have gone a little overboard when she had misted herself with expensive perfume and lathered tanning lotion on her legs, but it was too late to worry about that now. What was done was done. There was no going back. She just had to make sure that Andy Jenkins understood that her priority was Brandon.

Was she sorry she had come? No way. Brandon was worth whatever it took. This school had an excellent reputation and the best teachers. Why should she settle for second best in her son's life?

She watched as Mr. Jenkins shoved his fingers through his hair, standing it on end in the front. His hair spiking up in front gave him a youthful appearance. She couldn't stop the smile that turned up the corners of her mouth, the smile reaching all the way to her eyes as she surveyed the man who was going to help her son.

He was a man who could help Brandon make it through the fourth grade and beyond. She was sure of it. She knew in her heart that she could trust Andy Jenkins with her son.

She had read enough to know that some mothers were very possessive of their children, but she knew that Brandon would still need her, no matter what. There were some things only a mother could provide for a son. But there were other things a boy could only gain from male interaction. Brandon needed a male he could look up to.

She pushed away from the wall and made her way up the aisle, stopping a few feet away from the teacher.

"Are you willing to work a little with Brandon outside of class?" She deliberately kept her voice calm, despite her heart's jumping in anticipation.

When he continued to stare, she wanted to rush on, beg for his intervention, his time, his caring. One hand was clenched around her purse strap, the other at her side as she willed herself to stop talking and wait for his answer.

In Daddy's Shoes 45

He cleared his throat and took a step back, his legs bumping into the desk. Glancing quickly over his shoulder at the object in his way, he looked surprised that the desk was there, but he recovered quickly.

"Listen," he started, holding one hand out in front of him as if to keep her at a distance, "I haven't given this much thought, but . . ." He took a deep breath and allowed it to hiss out between pursed lips. "I could probably free up a few hours a week. But I'm just his teacher, and—"

"Wonderful!" Her enthusiasm splashed another hundred-watt smile across her face. "Somehow I knew I could count on you." Her words whispered out as tears clogged her throat.

When he glanced down at the hand she had impulsively placed on his arm, she recoiled, taking a step back.

"Oh, sorry," she stammered. "I'll be going now," she said, her quick smile disappearing as she turned toward the door. "Thank you so very much."

A half hour later she pulled into the driveway, pushing the garage-door opener clipped on the visor, halting the car until the door was fully up before easing into the crowded space and pushing the button again. She was singing along with the song on the radio, her heart suddenly light.

The alarm issued a signal when she opened the door to enter the house. In the rear of the house, in the direction of Brandon's bedroom, she heard loud music suddenly cease. She smiled as she walked down the hall to her bedroom. She had barely had time to set her purse on the hall table when she heard Brandon's voice behind her.

"Hi, Mom."

"Hi, honey." She turned to smile at her son. She stopped

when she saw him standing there frowning at her. "What's wrong?"

"Why are you dressed like that?"

She could hear the censure in his voice. Suddenly she felt like she was sixteen and her father was questioning the hemline of her skirt. He had been of the old school, thinking "good girls" didn't wear skirts above their knees.

"Didn't you go to work today?" Brandon persisted.

"Yes, I went to work," she said, one hand going to her hip as she returned his direct stare. "I had an appointment afterward," she hedged, "and I changed out of my work clothes."

"Why did you have to wear that? Why couldn't you just go in your suit? Who were you meeting?"

She had to stop this line of questioning. "I didn't realize I had to get your permission for the outing. Is your homework done?" she asked, changing the subject as she headed into her bedroom. As usual, Brandon followed her. They always used this time after work to tell each other about their day. She enjoyed the exchange and hoped Brandon didn't get too old to enjoy it anytime soon.

"Yeah, I only had spelling words, and they're easy." When she stopped and looked inquiringly at him over her shoulder, he continued. "I did the rest at school during lunch."

"Oh?"

"Yeah, ol' Mr. Jenkins is making me stay in at lunch all this week, since I missed last week," he said, his mouth quirking a little as he continued. "He said I needed the time to think about what I had done and to catch up on my

In Daddy's Shoes

studies. It's not fair, though, 'cause I turned in all my homework, and he still made me stay in," he grumbled.

Lydia smiled to herself to think that Andy . . . wait. When had he stopped being Mr. Jenkins? She shook her head, dismissing the thought, but she was glad to hear that the teacher had been working with Brandon even before she invaded his domain. After a moment she raised an eyebrow in a look that Brandon instantly understood.

"I don't want to hear you being disrespectful to your teacher or even talking that way about him to others. He brought your homework over here last Friday because he was concerned about you getting behind."

Even though Brandon shrugged, she knew he would curb his tongue—at least around her.

"Is that all he said?" She turned her back on him, toeing off her heels before heading to the closet to pull out jeans and a tank top. She turned her gaze to Brandon as she waited for him to answer.

"Yeah, well, he asked if I'd like to be on the football team or the baseball team."

"And?"

"I don't know," he mumbled, using the toe of one sneaker to trace a pattern in the carpet. "I mean, I don't know that much about football. I don't know all the plays, and I don't even know what part I'd want to play."

"What 'part'?"

"You know, what position. I think I'd like to be a quarterback and call all the plays, but I don't know them, so I guess I'd have to do something else," he concluded practically, finally looking up at his mother.

Her heart ached for her son. If Steven had been alive, she would bet that Brandon would be jumping all around the house, telling him about all the awesome plays he had made, and father and son would have been giving each other high fives over some play they had practiced that had turned out well on the field. For once she wished she had been more athletically than musically inclined. Well, she'd have to play the cards she had been dealt, and so would Brandon.

"I could be wrong, but I doubt the other boys know that much more than you this early in the season, and even if a few of them do, you're a quick learner, and I bet you'd make a great football player, just like your dad," she said, smiling at her son as he raised his head and connected with her level gaze.

"Do you really think so?" It looked like he was holding his breath.

She so wanted him to do well in life, and that meant that he would have to try new things and maybe even get knocked down a few times, but that was the only way to learn how to get back up.

She dropped the clothes onto the bed and walked over to her son. With her arms sliding around his thin shoulders to pull him close in a hug, she laid her cheek on his head.

"Yes, I really think so. In fact, I bet if you ask Mr. Jenkins, he just might know some of the plays and could get you caught up with the other boys in nothing flat." She pulled back to look into his face.

He was beaming for the first time in weeks. "Really?"

"Yep, I'd bet on it. Why don't you talk to him tomorrow at school and see if he has any free time?"

In Daddy's Shoes

"I doubt he'd want to spend his time with me," he hedged.

She smiled. "You never know unless you ask."

He shrugged and moved away from the door. "Okay," he mumbled on his way down the hall.

She had to smile as she hugged her joy to her heart. Things were starting to roll.

Chapter Six

It had been several days since Lydia had spoken with Andy Jenkins, but it wasn't as if she didn't know what he was doing. It seemed all Brandon could talk about now was Mr. Jenkins and how "cool" he was to spend time right after school to show him football plays and toss a few passes with him before the actual practice started.

Over the past couple of weeks her son had blossomed into quite an athlete, and she couldn't be happier. She tried to make it to the school each day in time to watch at least a portion of his practice, and today the sun was beating down on her shoulders, sending trickles of sweat down her sides. She couldn't imagine how hot the boys must be in their padding and helmets.

She had arrived at the field a little early and felt oddly let down when she saw Andy sitting beside one of the other mothers. She knew she didn't have a claim on the man, but somehow it rankled that she wouldn't have an opportunity to discuss Brandon's progress and thank him for all his help.

Lydia climbed up the bleachers, glancing toward where

the couple sat. She didn't really know the woman but had met her and spoken with her on a couple of occasions. All she knew was that her name was Connie and she had recently been divorced from her husband of twelve years.

She squirmed on the rough bench, wishing she had remembered her sunscreen, but mostly her mind was on the man and woman laughing and talking off to her right. It was Friday, and she was tired. She was looking forward to when the practice ended so she could take Brandon home, maybe order a pizza, and relax.

At that thought she saw Brandon get tackled and slammed to the ground, his helmet bouncing once before several other boys piled on top of him. She was on her feet in an instant, ready to run onto the field. Some invisible hand held her back as she heard the whistle blow and watched the boys scramble up, including Brandon. In an instant he was back in a huddle, getting instructions for the next play.

"Relax, Mom," came a male voice from beside her. She jerked her head around to see Andy standing on the ground beside the bleachers. She settled back onto the bench, pink as she laughed self-consciously.

"I've never watched him play sports before, and when all those boys piled on, I was sure he was going to be hurt," she admitted, shrugging.

"He's well padded, and he's doing fine." He smiled, swinging himself up onto the bleachers and stepping over her legs to sit down beside her.

"He's also learning the plays quickly and getting along well with all the other kids on the team, even though he came in a little late."

"Great. I was worried," she said, cringing as Brandon

grabbed one of the uniformed boys and dragged him to the ground.

"You know, the coach told me that he's a natural at sports. He has great coordination and good hands."

"What do you mean, 'good hands'?" She turned to look at him while the boys huddled again on the field.

"He has the ability to get his hands on the guy with the ball and hang on. He can also snatch a ball out of the air with precision. I was out here yesterday afternoon," he said, stopping a moment to yell out to a couple of the boys on the field.

"Go, guys! Greg, you're doing great! Hustle, John. Way to go!" When he turned back to Lydia, he chuckled. "They're in my class too. Anyway, back to Brandon. Coach said he's going to make him a pass receiver and that he's really surprised at his abilities, particularly since he never played before."

"His father was quite the all-around athlete. Maybe Brandon inherited some of his talent," she offered. She smiled in pride, but there was a pain in her heart as she thought about Brandon's father never getting a chance to see his son play football.

"Way to go, guys!" Andy stood as he cheered them on.

"You know," he said, sitting back down and giving her a quick glance before turning his eyes back toward the field, "first I was reluctant to get involved with Brandon outside the classroom. But I've been having a lot of fun . . . with all the guys," he quickly added.

"Come on, Charlie! Hustle!" he yelled out, cupping his hands around his mouth.

It was obvious to Lydia that Andy was encouraging all the kids. It touched a soft spot in her heart that they all got the benefit of his thumbs-up when they did well on a play. If she was totally honest, she'd have to admit that she found Andy Jenkins attractive in more ways than one.

Even as the thought crossed her mind, she moaned inwardly. What was wrong with her? She didn't need, nor did she want, a man in her life. She had enough on her plate with a boss who expected perfection and a son who had started to get into trouble. In just a week or so Brandon's self-esteem was showing signs of improvement, and she didn't want to do anything that might mess that up.

But she couldn't lie to herself. Just like a teenager, she had daydreamed about Brandon's teacher on more than one occasion. Several times lately she had returned home after practice with an empty feeling, like being the only one sitting at home on the night of the prom.

Well, she thought, *why not wallow a little more? Talk about feeling sorry for yourself!* She was disgusted with her mind playing a volleyball game with her emotions. The man was her son's teacher, and that was all. She had backed him into a corner and made him feel guilty so he'd help Brandon, and now she was disappointed with him for not falling at her feet. Regardless of her relationship, or lack of one, with him, she was thankful for Andy's help.

As they stood side by side and cheered on the players, a glow of contentment swept through her as she remembered back to a night not long ago that Andy had come by to talk with Brandon.

Brandon had raced to the front door when the bell rang. He peeked out the window, turning to her with a slightly confused look on his face.

"It's Mr. Jenkins. Why is he here?" His eyes narrowed.

"I've been doing my homework and behaving in class," he informed her. "Promise."

She almost laughed as he scowled. She knew exactly why Mr. Jenkins was there, and she only hoped that the teacher would be successful.

"I believe you, son. Why don't you open the door, and we'll both find out why he's here," she suggested.

It was obvious that Brandon wasn't eager to hear what the teacher had to say, as he continued to frown while he unlocked and slowly opened the door.

"Hi, Brandon. May I come in?"

The boy glanced back at his mother for her reaction, but all he got was a slight smile and a nod of her head.

"I guess," he muttered, stepping aside to allow the man to pass.

"Hi, Lydia. How are you this evening?" His smile was meant to encourage her, but her nerves were too close to the surface.

"I'm fine. Come on in. Can I get you a cool drink? Soda or iced tea?"

"Iced tea, if it's not too much trouble." He smiled again.

When she got to the kitchen, she quickly poured the tea so she could hurry back into the living room. She didn't want to miss anything. She wanted to hear Brandon's response, and she wanted to watch how Andy—Mr. Jenkins—dealt with the subject.

". . . I guess so."

"Well, the reason I asked is that Mr. Collins, the coach, was telling me the other day that he could sure use some more boys on the team. I was watching you throwing the football at recess today with Toby, and you're good."

In Daddy's Shoes 55

She was back in time to watch a broad smile creep slowly across Brandon's face as he basked in the praise.

"Well, it's up to you, but if you're interested, I'll see what I can find out about you joining the team."

Brandon lowered his head, his eyes darting quickly to his mother before he slowly shook his head. "No, that's all right," he said, his words spoken so softly that she could barely hear them.

"Did I hear you say that Brandon can throw a football well?" She set the tray on the coffee table and handed a glass to Andy.

"Yes."

She turned to look at Brandon. His head was still bowed; his hands with the chewed fingernails were picking at a thread on a worn knee of his jeans.

"You know, your father liked football and was pretty good at it. Don't you think you might enjoy playing on a team with the other boys in your class? In fact, isn't Toby on the team?"

His head snapped up to stare into his mother's eyes, a longing gaze that told her he was so hopeful yet so afraid she would tell him he couldn't play ball with the others.

"Do you want to play football?" From the look on his face she was sure she was asking a stupid question, but she wanted to hear his answer. She wanted to be sure that he was the one wanting to play, not going along with someone else's plan.

He nodded, swallowing as the look in his eyes turned to pleading.

Inside, her heart was quaking. She wasn't sure she wanted her son playing such a dangerous sport, but it would, after all, be with other young boys, and she knew she had to let him do it. Personally she would have preferred tennis or even baseball, but if football was what he wanted, then she would stand behind him all the way. She knew there was no way to keep him away from all the dangers in life, and he needed to learn everything he could about being a team member and taking responsibility.

She turned toward Andy and saw him watching her intently. She was sure he was reading her mind, but he remained quiet, not voicing his thoughts.

"What do we need to do for him to join the team?"

"Yippee!" Brandon was punching a fist into the air as he jumped up and twirled around. "I can't wait to tell the guys!"

The eruption was instantaneous and joyful. She flinched at the yell, but her heart swelled as she watched her son instantly go from sullen to elated. It was as if a switch had been flipped.

When the adults stopped chuckling, Andy answered her question.

"Well, you'll need to to fill out the forms, and he'll have to have a physical, but I think that's about it." He glanced at the boy who was now all smiles.

"Well, then, it looks like the team has a new member," she had announced, smiling broadly at her jubilant son.

Now Lydia stood watching the practice, and, regardless of how afraid she was that Brandon would get hurt, she was proud of him. He had been in a much better mood since joining the team. As Andy had predicted, he hadn't cut school, and he did his homework without being told.

It excited her that, instead of watching television in the

In Daddy's Shoes

evenings, he pored over the manual of plays, memorizing them and practicing his stance in his bedroom before charging forward to land on his bed.

Just the prior evening she had found Brandon in her room when she went in to put away folded laundry. When she walked in, he had been standing in front of her full-length mirror, decked out in his entire uniform, admiring how he looked. She had fought the urge to laugh and instead told him how tough and frightening he looked in all that gear. Through the face guard she could see that his smile stretched from ear to ear.

Her thoughts were jerked back to the present by a sultry voice.

"Hi, Andy," the ultra-feminine voice purred at Lydia's elbow. "Are you ready to go?" Connie's red lips were stretched into a confident smile.

Lydia wondered if the woman with the bouncy blond ponytail had ever been shy or unsure of herself.

Andy immediately stood, stopping to shake hands with Lydia.

"Well, tell Brandon that I'll see him in class on Monday and that I thought he did great out there today." He smiled, pulling his hand back and stepping down the bleacher until he was on the ground.

"See you later," called out Connie as she wiggled her fingers in a wave.

Lydia wondered if Connie had a son on the team and, if so, who was taking the child home if his mother was leaving with Mr. Jenkins.

Well, it was none of her business what arrangements parents made to get their children home, and it certainly didn't matter to her who Andy—Mr. Jenkins—dated. If he wanted to take the woman out for dinner or home for a drink, it was no concern of hers.

She lifted her chin a notch as she stared out at the football field. What he did was his own business. She had turned back to the game just in time to see Brandon catch a pass and run it in for a touchdown.

Chapter Seven

Andy was bored. He had asked Connie to dinner in the hope that going out with another woman would get his mind off Lydia. It wasn't working.

The woman talked too much. And she was too loud. He just wanted the evening to end, and she was making gentle hints that she wanted it to continue. No way. It had been a mistake to ask Connie out, and it was definitely time to take her home.

He found himself thinking about his class and about Brandon Reynolds in particular. He had thought that taking on Brandon was a mistake, but he was growing to really admire the boy. Brandon was polite and enthusiastic about life, despite how fate had robbed him of his father. Andy admitted to himself that he had hesitated to agree to help the boy because he had been slammed in the stomach with an invisible fist the first time he glanced up and saw Lydia Reynolds standing in the doorway. It wasn't the boy he was afraid of.

Brandon was doing better now—in fact, he was doing

great—so maybe he should start distancing himself. Being in proximity to Lydia was wreaking havoc with his concentration and his sleep. The woman was keeping him awake at night, and that had to stop.

"Andy? Did you hear me?"

He was jerked back to the restaurant and the woman sitting across from him. Devin Chi's was a nice, quiet little place, but he hoped the evening would end quickly. There was live entertainment scheduled in just over an hour—light jazz, and he really liked jazz—but he would have skipped it except that Connie had squealed, clapped her hands, and thanked him for bringing her, since she loved jazz.

Oh, brother. Now she thought he had done something special for her. Things weren't getting better. Instead, they were sliding downhill faster than a new sled. If only it were Lydia sitting across from him.

"I'm sorry, I didn't hear you. My mind drifted for a moment," he told her honestly, his lips quirking up in a half smile that he quickly erased when he remembered that she had told him that his smile was "cute."

Too late—Connie was already beaming and almost gushing as she reached over to take his hand.

"Oh, that's all right. It's been a long day, and I'm sure you're tired. If we go back to my place later, I can give you a massage to relax you," she told him, leaning in close to whisper her offer.

Andy averted his eyes to avoid staring at the cleavage on display before him as she leaned close.

"Oh, um, I have to be up very early tomorrow. After the first music set is over, I'm going to need to take you home," he rushed to tell her, his words falling out in a tumble.

In Daddy's Shoes

The woman sat back, tossing her long blond ponytail over her shoulder, while her bottom lip protruded playfully. She might have wanted to give the impression that she was teasing about being upset, but he could tell it wasn't a joke. He was sure she was disappointed that the evening wasn't ending up as she had hoped.

"How about a rain check?" he said vaguely, hoping not to hurt her feelings. When he looked at Connie, all he thought about was Lydia; all he wanted was for Connie to be gone and Lydia to be in her place. It wasn't fair to Connie.

How had Brandon's mother gotten under his skin so quickly? She wasn't even trying, for crying out loud. She never looked as if she had spent an hour dressing up and putting on makeup to impress him—well, except for that one time when she had come to his classroom.

No, she was either a lady through and through, or she just wasn't interested in him. That brought his thoughts to a jarring halt. Of course, he wasn't really interested in her either, he rationalized. With two dozen ten-year-olds distracting him from the pain of his divorce, he didn't need any extra distractions in his life right now. He had too much on his plate as it was, and he wasn't looking for a steady girlfriend.

He smiled unconsciously as he thought about how juvenile that sounded, as if he were back in high school.

"Andy, you have such a cute smile," Connie purred again. "Sure, I'll give you a rain check . . . for whenever you're available." She spoke softly, one sculptured red nail lightly trailing down his arm toward his hand. He watched its progress, mesmerized as it reached his hand. She slid her hand under his, turning her wrist to link their fingers. She squeezed, clinging to his hand as she inched her chair closer.

"Isn't this cozy?" She was near enough for him to smell the heavy fragrance she had used. He thought about swampy jungles and panthers stalking their prey through the underbrush.

He managed to silence the groan that threatened to slip out. What in the world was he doing here when all he wanted to do was run for cover? Connie seemed desperate, on the prowl. She had been divorced only a couple of months, and already she was looking for her next victim. *Victim?* Where did that thought come from? Well, whatever. He knew he didn't want to be the next entrée on her menu.

"Is something wrong, Andy? You don't look well." She leaned back enough to look into his eyes.

"I'm fine, just tired," he said.

He wasn't sure what she was seeing when she stared so intently at him, but she slowly pulled away from him, sliding her hand away from his.

"You're not interested." It wasn't a question. She could apparently tell that she had hit the nail on the head.

"Look, Connie," he said, lowering his eyes for a moment to look at his hands resting on the table before forcing his gaze to reconnect with her. "I like you—don't get me wrong—but I'm not interested in that kind of relationship at this time. I've got a lot going on, and I just don't have time to do justice to you . . . or anyone else, for that matter."

He didn't want to hurt her feelings, but he *wasn't* interested in her. He was mentally kicking himself for even asking her out. It wasn't fair to have used her to try to get someone else off his mind.

In Daddy's Shoes

"I'm sorry. I can take you home." He knew it was blunt, but he didn't know any other way to get out of the mess he had made. He had ruined the evening for her, and he was sorry, but the only thing he could do now was to be honest with her.

Her expression had progressed through several changes—from confusion to disbelief to resignation to irritation. He had seen them all before, when he was married. *Damn.*

Her eyes narrowed, and her jaw clenched. "Don't worry about me. I'm a big girl, and I'll find my own way home." With that, she stood and stalked toward the door of the restaurant, her purse slung over her shoulder to bump against her hip as she made her way through the tables.

He felt like a rat. But he also felt relief. That particular weight was now off his shoulders, and he leaned back, took a deep breath, and heaved a quiet sigh.

He glanced at his watch. Almost nine o'clock. "I wonder if it's too late to call Lydia," he murmured as he caught the eye of the waitress and mouthed the words to let her know he wanted the check.

"Mom, I'm not tired, and it's Friday," Brandon pleaded, wanting to stay up to play the new Xbox game he had saved his allowance to get.

"You had a long day with school and practice out there in the heat. Besides, you're a growing boy and need your sleep," she reasoned.

She had to smile when she heard a moan that sounded just like his father. Her mind wrapped around the memory of her disagreeing with Steven and him groaning with theatrical exaggeration until he made her laugh. That usually ended the discussion. Their disagreements never materialized into fights.

She felt her resolve slipping. He was only asking for half an hour more. She glanced at her watch. It was only nine o'clock, and, after all, he was right about it being Friday. She could let him sleep in the next morning, and there wasn't even a football practice the next day.

Why not? He had been behaving, doing his work, and deserved a reward.

"Okay, partner. Half an hour longer and then you scoot to bed without any arguments. Agreed?" Her hand was stretching out to shake on the deal when the doorbell rang.

Her head jerked around to glance toward the front door. "Who could be here this late in the evening?"

"I'll get it!" Brandon was already on his feet and launched toward the front door before she thought to say anything.

"Don't open the door. Ask who it is first," she instructed.

"Who is it?"

"It's Mr. Jenkins," came the muffled answer.

Without waiting for permission, Brandon flipped the lock and swung open the door.

"Hi, Mr. Jenkins." He beamed, grabbing the man by the hand and pulling him into the house.

Lydia wasn't sure what to say. She knew he had left the school with Connie, and here he was, a few hours later, standing in her entryway, smiling at her son as if he was as happy as a lark.

"Mom! It's Mr. Jenkins," he needlessly told her, his grin taking up most of his face. He turned back to the tall man standing beside him.

In Daddy's Shoes 65

"Come in," she said, smiling broadly. "What brings you by"—she glanced at her watch—"at this hour?"

Andy hadn't thought about why he had stopped, and he certainly hadn't thought up an explanation. "Um, I was in the neighborhood and saw your lights on, so I decided to drop in and . . . and see how the rest of the practice went after I had to leave," he finished up, glancing down at Brandon.

"It was great. Did you see the touchdown I made?" When the man shook his head, Brandon's face lit up at the opportunity to tell him what had happened.

"Before you get started on the play-by-play, would you two like something to drink?" She hated how excited she felt, how fast her heart was beating just because a man was here to visit. Well, it wasn't that it was just any man, but it was the man who had been on her mind all evening. Unfortunately, after watching him leave her side to walk away with Connie, she couldn't say that every thought had been complimentary, but she was willing to forget about Connie if he was.

"Iced tea, Mom."

"A glass of iced tea or soda would be fine, thank you." His eyes never wavered from hers until she headed for the kitchen.

Even as she turned her back to him, she gave a triumphant grin. Andy and Connie might have gone for a drink or even to eat, but now he was at her place, not Connie's. It felt good to open the refrigerator door and allow time for her flushed cheeks to cool. She also needed a moment or two to wipe the silly grin off her face.

What was wrong with her? She felt like it was the first time a boy had come to her house to see her. Worse yet, she didn't even know for sure if Andy was here to see her or to talk with Brandon about football. That thought brought her down to earth with a jolt.

She quickly got three glasses down, filled them with ice, and poured in the amber liquid. As she reentered the living room, she had to swallow several times at the scene before her so she wouldn't have tears overflowing her eyes.

In front of the television, Andy and Brandon were sitting on the sofa together, each with a set of controls, fighting the enemies in one of Brandon's games. As the sounds exploded from the television, she stood frozen to the spot at the palpable reminder that Brandon's father would never be able to play games with his son. He had missed out on the fun of watching Brandon grow into a sturdy little boy.

It also saddened her that Brandon had never had the chance to really know his father and do all the things that fathers and sons did together. Instead, Andy was helping out, for the moment taking Steven's place at her son's side. As sad as it was on the one hand, she was thankful and pleased that Brandon was responding so well to the man's attention.

Her mind darted fearfully into the future as she set the glasses on the coffee table and hovered on the edge of the recliner to watch the two males work together to defeat their foes. How would it affect Brandon when this man was no longer his teacher and no longer came over to spend time with him? How would she explain it to her son? Would it make it hard for him to trust in the future? Would he lose faith in adults because they all seemed to eventually leave?

In Daddy's Shoes 67

She slid back into the chair, her fingertips touching her lips as she concentrated on what she should do. Had she created a situation that would eventually hurt her son?

"Yeah!" Brandon and Andy grinned at each other as the boy bounced up and down on the seat cushion. "We did it! Mom and I never win." His eyes shone like lanterns as he gazed up at the man sitting next to him. "Can we play again?"

"Not this time," Andy told him, setting down the control. "But I sure enjoyed it. You're really developing good hand-and-eye coordination."

"You really think so?" So much hope shone out of the child's eyes that Lydia had to shut her own eyes for a moment, praying that Andy's words were true. Brandon's ego needed the compliment, but only if it was true.

"Brandon, here's your iced tea, and then you need to get to bed."

"Ah, Mom, can't I stay up, since Mr. Jenkins is here? I'll be quiet," he pleaded.

"No. I've already allowed you to stay up past your bedtime as it is, and you know we have plans for tomorrow afternoon, so you need your sleep."

"Oh." He whirled back around and looked up at Andy. "Tomorrow we're going to the lake to fish and have a picnic. Do you want to come with us? I'm sure Mom won't mind." His eyes were pleading as he shifted his weight from one foot to the other while he waited for the man's answer. "Please?"

"It's up to your mother," Andy hedged, silently thanking the boy for wanting to include him. Andy turned toward Lydia, knowing he was putting her on the spot yet not caring.

He wanted to spend the day with the two of them tomorrow, and he was willing to put her on the spot. After all, turnabout was fair play.

Her head was slightly bent, but she looked up at him through her lashes, a smile finally starting to show. As if she had been fighting an inner battle and had just come to a decision, she raised her chin and smiled broadly.

"Sure. We'd love for you to come with us. In fact"—she laughed—"I'll let you two be in charge of baiting the hooks, and I'll be in charge of the fried chicken and potato salad. Is it a deal?"

He loved her laugh—it sounded like a wind chime being gently moved by a breeze—but it was her eyes that held his attention. They had darkened, almost smoldering as she invited him to join them for the day. Her small hands were clutched around the damp glass of tea, her knuckles turning white, but her smile was genuine, her offer sincere.

He released the breath he had been holding while he waited for her response after Brandon's outburst. "Yes, it's a deal. I love to fish, and I'd enjoy spending the day with the two of you." He smiled at her before putting a hand on Brandon's shoulder and squeezing.

"In fact, I'll even clean any fish we catch, as long as you'll do the cooking." He held a hand over his stomach. "I'm not that great a cook, and I'd hate to ruin the fish," he admitted, a chuckle rumbling from deep within his chest.

He watched her gaze drop, but her smile remained. He liked everything about the woman. Sure, at first he had thought she was kind of pushy, but every time he was around her lately, he became surer than ever that deep down she was really shy. How she had gotten the nerve to pressure him for help for her son truly amazed him. She was one devoted, determined mom.

He wasn't sure what to do or say next, now that she was sending Brendan to bed. He couldn't believe that he had been handed an excuse to see her again so soon. Heck, he had a date with her in less than twelve hours, he thought. Well, not actually a real date, but a chance to spend time with her and Brandon. He guessed that the appropriate thing was to leave.

"Well, it's getting late, and I should be going," he said, taking a last swallow of tea and standing. He reached out his hand, and she placed hers in it to shake.

"Brandon," he said, turning to the boy, "great game. We'll have to do it again sometime soon." They also shook hands, Brandon standing straight and tall, excited to be included in the adult ritual.

"Sure," he beamed, all smiles now that he had gotten what he wanted.

"I'll see you both tomorrow." He started toward the door before stopping to turn back for a moment. "I almost forgot to ask what time," he said, looking once more into her eyes.

"Oh, um, how about ten o'clock? That will give us time to fish for a little while before lunch," she suggested, looking between the two males standing in front of her.

"Sounds good. I'll be here. See you tomorrow." He smiled one more time before bumping fists with Brandon.

Before she knew it, he was out the door, and she was standing at the window watching his pickup truck pull away from the curb.

"Mom?"

"Hmm?"

"What are you looking at?"

"Oh," she said, jerking around to look at her son. "Nothing." She motioned with one hand that he should head to his room. "Off to bed, soldier. We have a big day ahead of us tomorrow."

Even as he jogged down the hall toward his bedroom, she stood rooted to the spot.

Why had Andy come by? He had said it was to check on the practice, but somehow she didn't believe him. Did he want her to know that he had ended the evening early with Connie? A smile bloomed as she closed her eyes and hugged that thought to her chest. Could he really be interested in her? A woman with a ten-year-old son?

"Don't get your hopes up. He might have just not wanted to go home to an empty house so early in the evening." She could certainly understand that feeling. Whenever her parents had kept Brandon overnight, it had been hard to go home to a quiet house. Her parents had been trying to give her a break, give her a rest, but all it had done was amplify her loneliness and make her sad.

But tonight Brandon had been happy. In fact, he had been happier than she had seen him in a long time. She hadn't missed his mile-wide smile and the sparkle in his eyes. It was wonderful to see her son be excited about his day.

Warmth she couldn't explain accompanied her down the hall to Brandon's room. All was right with her world.

Chapter Eight

Brandon had reached the age where he didn't really want a good-night kiss. He gave her a quick hug before getting into bed but skipped the kiss as often as possible. Where had her little baby gone?

But tonight was different. He actually kissed her on the cheek and thanked her for letting Mr. Jenkins come fishing with them the next day. It warmed her heart and turned her to mush. Still, she was able to administer a mild warning.

"You're welcome, but next time, son, you need to ask me *first* before inviting someone to go with us," she admonished.

"Don't you want Mr. Jenkins to come with us?" He had climbed into bed but was now sitting up in the middle, the blankets draped across his lap. His attention was squarely on her, intently waiting for her answer.

"It isn't that I don't want him to come. I just want you to follow the same rules with Mr. Jenkins as I request of your other friends. You need to get my permission first, that's all," she concluded, watching him flop back on the bed before turning his high-voltage smile toward her.

"Won't it be neat to have him along?" He looked happier than she had seen him in a long time. It tore at her heart that he had been suffering, silent and alone with his thoughts, for goodness knew how long, and she hadn't noticed. She had been too focused on her own loss, her own obligations, and had missed the signs that Brandon needed help coping with life.

"Yes, honey. You two should have a great time. Now get to sleep," she instructed, pulling the blanket up over him before reaching over to ruffle his hair. "I have to get the chicken out of the freezer and boil the potatoes for the salad, so get a good night's sleep, and I'll see you in the morning." She kissed his forehead, standing to smile down at the boy who looked so much like his father. "Good night, honey."

She headed for the door as he called out to her. "Don't forget to pack the pickles. Mr. Jenkins loves dill pickles," he informed her.

"All right." So he loved dill pickles. She could add that to the list of things she was learning about the amazing teacher who had invaded her thoughts and dreams ever since she met him.

She had to smile when she thought about Brandon's wondering if she wanted Mr. Jenkins to go fishing with them. She wanted Andy to come with them more than she could ever admit to her son. Unfamiliar emotions were bombarding her day and night, emotions that she thought had died forever with her husband. At Steven's funeral she was in such an emotional pit, she felt she would never be able to climb out. Her life had come to a screeching halt. She

In Daddy's Shoes

had hit a brick wall and had been a wreck for some time after that horrible day.

Now, only two years later, she wasn't sure how to handle the feelings she was having for this man she had dragged into her son's life and ultimately into her own. He wasn't Hollywood handsome, but he had a lopsided smile like Harrison Ford's that made her toes curl. He wasn't a parent yet himself, but he was great with kids.

She stopped in the kitchen to close her eyes and wrap thoughts of him around her like a cloak, flushing slightly as she imagined what it would be like to kiss him.

When she opened her eyes, she realized she was staring blankly toward the refrigerator, grinning like Goofy. What had she come in here for? It took a moment for her to remember that she needed to get food ready for the picnic the next day.

"This is crazy," she whispered aloud, shaking her head and yanking on the handle of the freezer. Even after the door had swung open, she stood staring for several seconds at the various packages as the mist rolled out into the warm room before she blinked and focused enough to get out the chicken. "I practically steamrolled him into helping Brandon, for goodness sake, and now I've cast him as my leading man," she said, tossing the chicken into the kitchen sink.

She put both hands on the edge of the sink, bowing her head to think. She had to get a grip on her emotions. He was Brandon's teacher, a male mentor for her son. He hadn't signed on for anything else, so she had to stop thinking of him as the answer to all her prayers. He was in her life because she had goaded him into helping Brandon. That was it. No other reason. For all she knew he only tolerated her. *Ouch.* But sometimes the truth hurt. That was life. Isn't that what she had told Brandon on numerous occasions?

It was after eleven before the potato salad was finished and in the refrigerator to cool overnight. The chicken had thawed enough for her to season it and put into the refrigerator to wait until the next morning to be fried, but she was still restless. She tried to read, but it was useless. She wished she still had a piano. Playing was so relaxing. Oh, well. She sensed she was going to get very little sleep.

Lydia wasn't the only one awake late into the night. Brandon lay in bed running the evening over in his mind. He had started out the school year not liking Mr. Jenkins, but the more he got to know him, he had started to change his mind. It had been cool to play video games with Mr. Jenkins. His mom hated playing them, and whenever she finally gave in, she didn't do it right, and they always lost. They were killed so many times that it was embarrassing.

There was one thing that he needed to think about, though. Toby and a couple of the other guys had been teasing him that he was the teacher's pet because Mr. Jenkins had been coming to all the practices and helping Brandon learn the plays.

Even though Brandon had vehemently denied it, Toby kept razzing him about Mr. Jenkins' only being nice to him because he wanted to get to know Brandon's mother.

"That's crazy," he muttered into the dark room. But was it? Was Mr. Jenkins hanging around him because of his mom? Toby had asked if the two had kissed yet. How was he supposed to know? Why would anyone want to kiss

In Daddy's Shoes

his mom anyway? Adults always kissed on the mouth, and that made his breathing stop for a moment.

"Has Mr. Jenkins kissed my mom? On the mouth? Yuck," he whispered as he scrunched up his face and closed his eyes. He'd have to keep his eye on things. Toby had told him that if Mr. Jenkins kissed his mother, then that would be the sign.

Lydia was up early the next morning, frying the chicken and loading the picnic basket when she heard Brandon tromp down the hallway and barge into the kitchen.

"Hi, Mom," he yelled out as he swung open a cupboard to grab a bowl and his favorite box of cereal. She never allowed him to have any of the sugar-coated cereals, so his bowl was soon full of Cheerios.

As she watched him get the milk from the refrigerator and pour some onto his cereal, she decided not to remind him that she had given him Cheerios to snack on when he was a baby. She had a picture of him in his high chair, with Cheerios on two of his fingers as he reached toward the camera. Ah, the good old days, when life was hectic but somehow simpler.

"How long before Mr. Jenkins gets here?" Brandon asked. Milk dribbled down his chin as he talked with his mouth full.

When she frowned at him, he gave her a sheepish grin and shrugged.

"In about an hour and a half, so you have plenty of time to make your bed and straighten up your room after you finish your breakfast."

"Ah, Mom. Can't it stay messy for one day?"

"Do you really want to go fishing today?" She stood looking at his disgusted expression for an extra moment before turning back to the chicken.

"Yeah," he muttered, finishing the cereal and picking up the bowl to slurp up the milk. He kept his eye on his mother's back, since she didn't like that habit of his. But it just took too long to drink it one spoonful at a time.

When he set the bowl down, he zipped from the table, heading for his bedroom. Lydia turned to pick up his bowl from the table. She had watched his reflection in the glass-fronted cabinet as he drank the milk, but she'd let it go. Lately she felt like too much of a nag, and she didn't like the role.

By the time the doorbell rang, she had the picnic basket packed and was in her room putting on her tennis shoes.

"I'll get it!" She could hear Brandon running down the hall toward the front of the house.

She closed her eyes and took a deep breath. All she had to do was go out there, greet Andy as if he was just another one of her son's friends, and then spend the day with him. Oh, yeah, and she had to remember to act normal and not stumble over her feet while staring, openmouthed, at the man.

"Right. That's all I have to do today," she said, opening her eyes and squaring her shoulders. "Piece of cake," she muttered.

Andy stood on the porch, pausing to take a deep breath before reaching to ring the doorbell. Was he doing the right thing? Should he be getting so involved with one of his students? Especially one with such a beautiful, tempting mother?

In Daddy's Shoes

Before he could change his mind and retreat, he pushed the doorbell. He had made a decision. He admitted to himself that even if it wasn't a good idea, he was interested in Brandon *and* his mother. Lydia Reynolds might flick him away like a pesky bug if she knew, but he'd take things slowly and see what happened.

He heard Brandon call out that he was getting the door. Any second the boy would swing open the door to greet him. It made him feel good to have Brandon so excited to see him, It reassured him that he was doing a good job with the boy. If he could affect Lydia enough for her to be even half as excited when he came over, he might be able to get her to accept a real, pick-her-up-at-the-door date.

"Patience, Andy. Give her time to adjust to your being around, and maybe she'll start to miss you when you're not," he muttered, smiling as the front door swung open.

By the time they were ready for lunch, they had caught five fish among them. He had only needed to show Brandon once how to bait the hook and cast the line into the lake. The boy was sharp and watched every move like a hawk looking for dinner.

"So," Brandon started, crumbs from the crispy chicken falling into his lap, "when are we going to eat the fish?" He looked over at his mother, who quickly glanced away.

"Fish are best if they're eaten fresh instead of freezing them for later," Andy offered, keeping his eyes on his plate of food as he scooped up another bite of the best potato salad he had ever had. "Are there cucumbers in this?"

Lydia's laugh washed over him, drawing his eyes to her mouth. "I hope you aren't allergic to them. Yes, there's cucumber in it. Old family recipe," she admitted, forking up a mouthful for herself.

"No, I'm not allergic. In fact, this is probably the best potato salad I've ever eaten."

He knew he had to handle this situation with care. He didn't want to come on too strong or too fast. If he did, she might run the other way. On the other hand, he didn't want to lose the opportunity to spend the evening with this woman who had riveted his attention.

"Yeah, that was what I was thinking," agreed Brandon. He glanced from Mr. Jenkins to his mother. Both were staring down at their plates as if it took some high level of concentration in order to eat potato salad.

Lydia glanced at her son. "You think the potato salad is that good?"

"It's always good," he said. "But I'm talking about eating fish while they're fresh instead of freezing them for later. I agree with Mr. Jenkins," he clarified.

Silence hung like a fog for several seconds.

"So," Andy asked, looking up at Lydia, "why don't you two come to my place for dinner tonight, and we'll have a fish fry?"

"Yeah!" Brandon immediately agreed, obviously not wanting the day to end any sooner than it had to.

When the other adult remained silent, Andy took several slow breaths before prompting her to answer. "Well, Lydia, what do you think?" He knew he was putting her on the spot, but otherwise she might not agree to come. "Do you trust me to fry fish?" He waited until she raised her eyes before he smiled. He wasn't sure how she had burrowed

In Daddy's Shoes

under the walls that usually kept people, especially beautiful women, at a distance, but she had.

"Oh, I'm sure you'd do a great job of frying the fish, but we can't put you to that much trouble," she said, setting her chicken down and picking up a napkin to wipe her fingers.

"Aw, Mom," groaned Brandon.

"Now, Brandon, we can't impose any more on Mr. Jenkins. He's been nice enough to take us fishing, and we don't want to take advantage of his hospitality."

"But, Mom, he didn't bring us fishing. We brought him. So now he wants to pay us back by cooking for us. Wouldn't it be rude to say no?"

She was sure there was a smirk hiding just behind her son's lips, but he was smart enough to keep it hidden. Her son was bordering on what *her* mother would have called "sassy."

Not one to miss the opportunity to drive the point home, Andy spoke up. "Yeah, 'Mom.' It would be rude to refuse me, so just say, 'Yes, thank you, we'd love to come to your house and eat fish,'" he coaxed.

She silently pondered what to do. When she finally spoke, her face relaxed into a smile that reached her eyes and softened the frown lines across her forehead.

"Yes, thank you. We'd love to come to your house and eat fish," she mimicked.

It took only a moment for Andy to register her sense of humor and reward her with a grin. Brandon laughed so hard that bits of potato salad flew from his mouth, landing on the blanket.

"Brandon," she admonished, laughing while she cleaned up the mess he had made.

"Great," Andy said, picking up his chicken. "You can also check out my place so you can report back to all your friends about how clean your son's teacher keeps his house, even though he's a bachelor," he added just before taking a big bite and chewing as she laughed.

"Let me guess," she said as she chuckled. "You have a cleaning service, and they just came yesterday," she concluded.

"Right," he said, still chewing, "but if you tell anyone that part, I'll just have to deny it," he answered.

"You mean you'd lie?" Brandon had followed the conversation and saw this as his opportunity to get in on the fun.

"Not exactly," he hedged, laughing.

"Well, my mom says people should never, and I mean *never*, tell a lie. In fact, she punishes me double if she catches me telling a lie," he said, sounding slightly disgusted.

"Good for your mother. But I was only teasing her. We might joke about something, but in the end, we *should* always tell the truth." His look was serious but friendly as he reached over to ruffle the boy's hair.

"Man," he grumbled, "I'm getting it from both sides."

The adults both burst out laughing as they watched the boy frown.

After they had eaten their fill and the leftovers were packed away, Andy taught Brandon how to clean the fish before putting them on ice.

"Now that all the work is done, how about a short stroll along the path that goes around this end of the lake? I think

In Daddy's Shoes 81

it would help settle all the food we ate," he said, rubbing a hand across his flat stomach.

"Sure." She had been concerned about spending so much time with Andy, figuring she wouldn't know what to say, but his easy flow of stories and jokes had made the time fly. Besides, she loved walking through the trees, and early fall was her favorite time of the year.

After putting the basket and blanket in the truck, they headed toward the path that would take them through the trees that were turning beautiful oranges, yellows, and reds. The path encouraged them to take a leisurely pace, but Brandon darted ahead and only occasionally returned to walk with the adults. After he had stopped a few times to throw rocks into the lake, Andy showed him how to skim flat stones across the top of the water.

Lydia was unable to stop the tears that welled up in her eyes. The pair looked like father and son. But Brandon's father would never again get to share such moments with their growing boy.

Soon after Brandon was born, she and Steven had strolled the hospital corridor and stood outside the nursery window, gazing at their son as he slept. Steven had been so excited, his eyes sparkling, as he told her all the things he would teach their son one day. He had barely put a dent in the list before he had shipped out to Iraq.

Now as she watched her son, his confidence growing with each newly mastered skill, she was proud of the person he was becoming. She was sure he would do great things with his life when he was older. Then it occured to her that he might even follow his father into the military. Although that was an honorable path, the thought sent a shiver down her spine. She knew she would never be able to encourage him to choose that profession, but if he chose it on his own, she'd back him just as she had his father.

"Are you cold?" Andy had seen her shiver, seeming to withdraw into herself since he and Brandon had skimmed some stones. Had he unwittingly upset her, overstepped some boundary?

"No," she said, smiling gently up into his face. "I'm sorry. I was just thinking." They walked along in silence for a few minutes, watching Brandon climb up onto a big tree stump before jumping off and jogging down toward the lake to chase a duck.

"If we could just figure a way to bottle half of his energy and sell it, we'd be able to retire in style," he said with a chuckle, hoping to lighten the mood.

Andy had been trying to fight the attraction he felt for Lydia, but he was being drawn to her like a magnet to metal. He liked to see her smile and loved to hear her laugh. All day he had resisted the temptation to touch her, but now he was trying to figure out a way to casually take her hand or put his arm around her. Would she pull away?

At lunch he had sat near enough to her that her fragrance enticed him even over the fried chicken. It was a fresh scent, like soap or deodorant, and it was driving him crazy. It was a clean, simple fragrance he had come to associate with her.

The light breeze picked up the loose hairs that had escaped from her ponytail and blew them around her face. She had long, thin fingers that drew his gaze as she reached up to tuck the stray hairs behind her tiny ears. A small diamond stud sparkled in her earlobe as the sun reflected on

In Daddy's Shoes 83

it, drawing his eyes to one of the spots he would like to kiss. His stomach tightened at the thought. Would she push him away? Or would she draw him closer?

Even as he was telling himself that he had to get his thoughts off his desire—no, his *need*—to kiss this woman beside him, Brandon came racing back into view, reminding him that she had been married and that she was a widow.

Damn. How long did a woman need to grieve a dead husband? Was it too soon to ask her out? He'd have to call his sister and ask her. No, that was a bad idea. His sister would start to push him to marry the woman even before he had a chance to take her on more than half a dozen dates. No, he'd keep Marisa out of his relationship as long as possible. Of course, he'd have to *have* a relationship before he could keep his meddling sister out of it.

They walked along for several minutes before the silence was broken.

"I know it's none of my business, but I was wondering if you'd ever been married." Lydia flushed as she figured that he would think she was being too nosy. "I mean, you seem to be so good with kids that I figured you'd have a bunch of your own." She smiled up at him.

A chuckle blurted out before he could stop it. "No," he said, shaking his head, "I don't have any children of my own." He walked on in silence for a few moments before continuing. His voice was husky, as if it was a difficult subject. "I was married for a couple of years, and although it started out great and I thought we were both very happy, she was unfaithful, and it ended in divorce."

Even now, on a warm day in October with a slight breeze blowing through the trees to cool him, he could still feel the emptiness and the aloneness he had felt that day. Her betrayal had punched him in the stomach, leaving him unable to grasp the concept of having loved someone who could do that to him. Worse, he could still feel the hurt and the helplessness of the day a doctor had come to the waiting room to tell him that his wife had miscarried.

"Was that the *Reader's Digest* condensed version?" Lydia smiled cautiously as she glanced over at the brooding man.

He heaved out a big sigh, sheepishly smiling at her.

"I'm sorry. That wasn't fair. It's not a story I'm proud of. In fact, it reminds me just a bit of how you were so upset with yourself for not realizing that Brandon was so stressed out. You blamed yourself for being too busy to notice his pain, and that's kind of where I was with my wife." He paused, then continued.

"My younger sister introduced me to a friend of hers about five years ago, and Sheryl and I instantly hit it off. The only problem was that I only *thought* I knew her. I really didn't. We ended up getting married, but within a year she had cheated on me." He took a deep breath before continuing in a quieter voice as he looked back into history.

"She said she loved me, but I don't think Sheryl knows what love is. The marriage was doomed from the beginning, but we didn't realize it until it was too late. The final straw was when she got pregnant. She had a rough time during the pregnancy, she was always depressed, and then . . . then she miscarried."

They walked along for a few moments in silence before he continued. "I was devastated and fearful of how depressed she would become when she found out about losing the child. I was in the room when the doctor told her the baby was gone, and she actually admitted that she was relieved. She even told me that she had never really wanted to get pregnant again, never wanted to have another child, and she was going to make sure that she never got 'caught' again. She said she didn't want to get fat and ugly."

Lydia couldn't stop a gasp as she turned stricken eyes toward the man sharing such a personal part of his life with her. His head was down and his shoulders slumped as he took several breaths before continuing, his eyes reflecting the horror and pain she felt for him. She reached over to touch his arm in a comforting gesture, but he scarcely seemed to notice.

"That night in the hospital, I stood at the foot of her bed watching her sleep and realized that I was married to a stranger. She had taken my love and loyalty and ground them into the dirt. When the part of me growing inside her died, she wanted to celebrate. Can you believe that? I thought I knew the woman."

"Before I married Brandon's father, we discussed not only how large a family we wanted but how soon to start. Didn't you ever discuss children with Sheryl?" Lydia asked softly.

"I guess I just assumed that every woman wanted children," he admitted with a sheepish shrug. "I don't know. When I met Sheryl, I only saw the beautiful, sexy, fun woman and overlooked the person who always put herself first. When I look back, I can't believe I was blind to what she wanted out of life, instead assuming she wanted the same things I did." He shook his head in bewilderment as he turned to look at her. "That was pretty selfish of *me,* actually."

"I'm so sorry," she told him. "But I have to say, you don't strike me as selfish in the least. Far from it," she assured him. Her heart was pounding as she contemplated someone not wanting her own child. She couldn't imagine how she'd feel if she miscarried a child, but she knew she would never react the way Andy's wife had. She couldn't imagine life without her beloved Brandon, regardless of her circumstances.

"After that we didn't seem to have anything in common," Andy said quietly. "We couldn't even seem to talk anymore. I suddenly realized that all she wanted to do was go out dancing and partying, and all I wanted was to have children and make a family. We grew so far apart that neither of us could see us ever coming back together. Finally we agreed to file for divorce."

"Did she ever remarry?"

"Oh, yeah, she did. She met and married a guy almost twenty years older than her. He's a big-shot broker, and they live in Manhattan. I think that's more the lifestyle she wanted. She sent her son from her first marriage to year-round boarding school, so she's happy now that she doesn't have to worry about kids. The guy has grown children of his own, and they're both happy to just enjoy the party life together."

"You know, she was actually lying to you if she knew what you wanted out of life and didn't bother to discuss it with you until after your marriage."

"Yeah, I guess that's true. I hadn't looked at it quite like that. I just had a difficult time with the fact that she could

In Daddy's Shoes 87

lie to me as easily as telling me it was time for dinner. Try as I might, I knew I would never be able to trust her again."

They walked on as his mind relived leaving the hospital after Sheryl lost the baby. He had been stunned, walking for miles in a daze without even knowing where he was going, not knowing how he would ever reassemble what he'd thought would be his life. Ultimately, his chosen profession had proved an enormous boon, allowing him to contribute in a meaningful way to future generations.

"So, have you dated anyone seriously since?"

"No. It's been almost three years, and so far being a teacher to other people's kids seems to suit me." They walked along in silence, each with their own thoughts.

As he watched Brandon running and jumping, he wondered again what his life would have been like if his own child had lived. Would it have been a little girl who loved to climb trees and ride her bike? Or maybe a boy like Brandon who would have looked up to him to teach him how to clean fish? He felt the tension gripping his chest as tears pooled behind his eyes. He cleared his throat and ordered himself to stop wallowing. He might not be able to change the past, but he could certainly try to make the future better.

Lydia's heart was aching for this caring compassionate teacher who had lost his own child. That must have nearly killed him. They walked along in silence, each with their own shadows from the past to darken their day. Finally, she decided to change the subject and try to get Andy to smile. It was too beautiful a day to linger any longer in the past.

"You know," Lydia said, staring up at the sky that peeked through the trees, "I love walking in the woods. I love the sounds and the smells," she said, stretching her arms out to encompass the area around them. "It's so peaceful, so quiet," she concluded, turning a bright smile in his direction. "You've been quiet for the past few minutes, and I almost hesitated to interrupt your thoughts."

"It's a welcome interruption," he acknowledged. "I was walking down a path that wasn't very happy, and I don't want to ruin today by thinking about a time of my life that I can't do anything to change."

He inwardly debated for another moment before tossing caution to the wind. On impulse, he reached over to take her hand, holding it as they continued to walk. She didn't pull away. His fingers linked with hers, their arms gently swinging back and forth as they strolled down the pine-needle-covered path.

When Andy's hand touched hers, tingles shot up Lydia's arm, and warmth invaded her entire body. She was shocked but thrilled that he had taken a step to bring them closer. It was all she could do to keep her imagination from running wild.

Was this his way of trying to tell her that he liked her? She didn't want to jump to any wrong conclusions and read too much into the casual touch of their hands. Had he held Connie's hand on their date?

She didn't like that thought at all. She made the mental choice not to think about him with another woman and just concentrate on the two of them today. Somehow the day was suddenly brighter, the trees greener, and the late-blooming flowers more fragrant. It might have been her imagination, but it felt wonderful.

Oh, it was so nice just to feel happy and carefree again. For just a few minutes she didn't want to think about where

In Daddy's Shoes

holding hands with this man might take her. For once she didn't want to have to think or act like an adult. She just wanted to feel the excitement without worrying about what came next.

Andy was quiet for a few more minutes before he looked down and squeezed her hand. When she turned her face toward him and smiled, his answering smile melted her insides.

As they strolled, she was suddenly fifteen again, remembering her first crush. Richard Danskin, the basketball team captain with a reputation for having a different girlfriend every week. He had held her hand in the bleachers at a football game under the blanket they had spread across their legs. It was one of those "secret" relationships where she told all her friends, but he told no one. It had lasted less than a week before he broke her heart by holding Lisa Miller's hand while walking to class one day, right in front of all her friends, announcing to the world that he was proud to be seen with her.

That had really shaken her confidence until Steven, tall and good-looking with his dimpled left cheek, had asked her to the movies. He was a year older and had a car. She had gone out with him, and the rest was history. It seemed so long ago.

"Do you want to talk any more about your past?" She tilted her head, trying to look into his eyes. She didn't want to intrude, just be available as a friend.

"No, not really," he told her, smiling briefly to take the edge off his blunt response. "I've already said more than I intended. I don't want to ruin the fun we've been having today." He squeezed her fingers and changed the subject.

"Okay, we'll talk about the trees and the flowers or something," she suggested with a determined nod of her head. "We'll stay away from politics, religion, and our pasts. Agreed?"

"Agreed."

"Have you noticed that a breeze is coming up? It's gotten a little cooler. Do you think we should turn back?"

"If you're chilled, I can keep you warm," he offered, moving his eyebrows up and down while he twisted an imaginary mustache. "All you have to give me in return is the deed to the ranch." He leered.

It felt good to laugh together.

They walked along in easy silence until she was sure Brandon was too far away to hear her ask the question that had been costing her sleep for the past couple of weeks.

"Andy, how do you think Brandon is doing lately?" When he didn't speak right away, she rushed on. "I know he's doing his homework, and he loves being on the team, but how do you think he's *really* doing? Emotionally, I mean."

He felt her grip on his hand tighten as she waited for his answer. He wasn't sure how much more of his background he wanted to share just now, but it might help her to know that he had once walked in Brandon's shoes.

He heaved a sigh before turning his head to glance at her while they walked. "When I was twelve, my family had been out to a county fair, and we were on our way home when a drunk driver crossed over the center line and slammed into the driver's side of our car." He held one hand up to stop her from saying anything.

"One day I was hitting balls with my father, and the next he was dead. Just like that," he said, snapping his fingers.

In Daddy's Shoes

"Anyway, my mother and I were injured but lived. My younger sister had stayed with relatives for the night, so she wasn't in the car. My mother was in the hospital only a week. I was there for two with broken bones and a concussion. My mother and father had been so in love, and suddenly she was alone, with full responsibility for an angry twelve-year-old and a confused five-year-old." They walked along in silence for a few moments before he continued.

"Looking back, I know she struggled, and I'm sure she cried herself to sleep many nights. But she was great, and ultimately she got me involved with a man from our church who was willing to spend some time with me. I started out resenting him; he wasn't my father and could never take his place," he admitted. Then he shrugged.

"Were you angry with the world too? Did it affect your schoolwork? Your behavior?"

He barked out a short laugh. "I was mad at everyone and everything. God, teachers, my mother—everyone and everything," he repeated. "I took it out on anyone who crossed my path."

"What turned you around?"

"My mom's patience with me helped, and the church guy did too. Then, when I was about sixteen, I had a gym teacher who sort of took me under his wing. I respected him more than anyone I knew at the time. One day he sat me down and told me exactly what he thought of my attitude and where I was headed in life. Then he simply sat across the desk from me and asked me if that's where I wanted to go or if I was going to get my head screwed on straight. He must have been the president of the tough-love club, because he didn't spare my feelings. It was just what I needed at that point in my life, because the next thing I knew, I was marching to a different drummer."

"I'm sure it wasn't that easy," she murmured, thinking about Brandon.

"Not easy but necessary. All of it," he acknowledged.

They walked on for a couple of minutes, watching Brandon in the distance as he stopped to skim some stones across the lake before heading back toward them in a gangling lope.

"The good thing is that Brandon is young and basically a happy kid. I think he'll make it if you just hang in there and keep doing what you're doing with him."

Lydia started to pull her hand away from Andy's when she realized that Brandon's eyes were glued to that link between the two adults. Just as quickly she felt Andy squeeze tighter, not allowing her to slip away without making an issue and having a tug-of-war.

"Hi, what's up?" Brandon's eyes moved from their hands to glance between the two of them, waiting for an answer.

"Nothing much. Are you having a good time?"

"Yeah." He still looked wary of what was happening between his mother and Mr. Jenkins. "Why are you guys holding hands?"

"When guys get older, they hold hands with girls they like, and I happen to like your mother. Is that okay with you?" Andy said easily.

They had stopped, but Lydia's heart was pounding as if she had run a marathon. This could be a defining moment. How would her son react to Andy's question?

He hesitated for only a couple of moments before shrugging. "It's okay, I guess."

She silently released the breath she had been holding. She had an almost giddy feeling of relief as she glanced at Andy, returning his smile with a nervous little twitch of her lips. She was over one hurdle, but the rest of the race was still ahead of her.

Chapter Nine

The evening traffic was at a standstill. For the past ten minutes the cars hadn't moved. Thank goodness it was a cool day, not sweltering like in the summer. Instead of turning up the radio to hear if there had been an accident, Lydia turned it down a little lower. She didn't care how long it took to get home. She was just going to enjoy the solitude and take the opportunity to wander through her memories of the past few weeks.

Each day when she got off work, she rushed home to hear about her son's day, and every day he had new stories to tell her. It thrilled her to hear the excitement in his voice as he told what Mr. Jenkins had said or done in class or about some great play he had made during practice. Brandon was happy. Life was good.

She lingered over the memories of Andy holding her hand at the lake and the one time he had almost kissed her. If they hadn't heard Brandon coming, she might have another memory to tuck into her heart. She might have had the memory of Andy's lips on hers to pull out at night to mull over and savor.

The only problem was that Andy seemed to draw near at times and then pull away. After the day at the lake, he hadn't gotten close to her, hadn't touched her, and had barely talked to her over the past week. He had spoken to her only once, and that was when she had called to tell him that she had to work late and asked him if he could drop Brandon off at home.

Even though he had offered to bring him home any day she couldn't make it to practice, he had maintained his distance. Last evening when he pulled up in front of the house, Brandon jumped out, waved, and Andy drove off.

She still felt the disappointment. She had been sure he'd walk Brandon up to the house and she would have a chance to invite him in for a cup of coffee or something.

Today she had been really late leaving work, and now, with the traffic delays, she was running even later. Brandon would be home already, and she hoped he had followed the rules and finished his homework.

Well, if he hadn't, she'd cut him some slack. It was Friday, and he had two days to get it done, she told herself, turning down her street. There were kids outside tossing a football, but Brandon wasn't with them.

Two whole days with her son. She was looking forward to having time to relax with Brandon, to talk about how school and football were going and how he was feeling about life in general. Maybe they could even go to a movie or out for pizza.

She paused for a moment to analyze the feelings jetting

through her. Yep, she had to admit that she was more excited about each new day than she had been in a very long time. The anticipation of maybe seeing or talking with Andy also put a new bounce into her step and a more contented smile onto her face.

Even her co-workers had noticed. They had been asking her if she had a new boyfriend.

By the time she reached her house at the far end of the street, she was humming along with the soft music from the radio, her fingers playing piano riffs on the steering wheel.

She turned into their driveway, pushing the garage door opener clipped to her visor. She glided in, closed the garage door, jumped out of the car, and headed for the door leading into the house.

Even though the kitchen looked the way she had left it that morning, there was something about the house that seemed different. It was too quiet. As if no one was home. Had practice run over?

She dropped her purse on the dinette table and glanced at the phone on her way by, but no message awaited.

She already knew she wouldn't find Brandon in his room, but she looked anyway. His bed was unmade, and his backpack had been tossed onto the foot, where it lay on its side. Everything else looked the way it did every afternoon. Total chaos.

Lydia knew she had to stay calm. There was no reason to panic, but she was unable to stop her heart rate from spiking.

Had Brandon been hurt at practice? No, Andy would have called her.

She raced through the house, grabbing her purse as her

trembling fingers dug out her cell phone and punched the button for Andy's home. She had never been good at waiting, and as she listened impatiently to the five rings, fear was already gripping her stomach and turning it into knots. There was no relief when she heard Andy's voice telling her to leave a message at the beep.

"Hi, Andy, it's Lydia. Listen, it's almost six o'clock, and Brandon isn't home yet. Do you know where he is? I'll be out looking for him, so please call me on my cell phone. Thanks." She flipped the phone closed. "Dear God, please take care of my little boy," she whispered even as she was turning to head back out to her car.

She punched in the number of Andy's cell phone just before jamming her foot onto the accelerator, jetting down the driveway and into the street. She had heard once that God looked out for children and fools. She hoped that was true. Just before shoving the gearshift into drive, she punched the send button, and as she accelerated, pushing her back into the bucket seat, she punched the speaker button so she could hear without holding the phone to her ear. After three rings she left the same message, adding a plea for him to please hurry.

She checked the football field and the playground next to the school and then drove to the park in town where she had taken Brandon on numerous occasions. Her nerves were unraveling as she stopped at the house of the last of his friends who lived within bike-riding distance of their home.

Her next stop was Andy's house. As she pulled into the driveway, she noticed that his next-door neighbor was out watering her flowers, but she disregarded the woman as she headed for the front door and rang the bell.

After several tries, she gave up and headed back toward her car. As she approached, the neighbor waved.

"He's not home. He usually goes to the pub for pool on Friday nights." The woman was slightly bent over and had on jeans, gloves, and a light jacket. A breeze tickled the wisps of white hair around her weathered face and neck. She was at least eighty but looked full of energy, a twinkle in her eye as she instructed the younger woman how to find her unmarried neighbor.

"Which pub is that? Do you know?"

"Sure, dearie. The same one he and his buddies always go to. Little Andy has lived next door to me since he was this high," she said, holding her hand below her waist to indicate a short person. "Well," she added, "he left for a few years after he married that woman, but when he came to his senses, he moved back," she said, starting to spray her flowers again.

"Could you give me the name of the pub?" She didn't want to be rude and rush the woman, but Brandon was out there somewhere, and she needed to find him.

"Sure, dearie. You go to the end of this street"—she pointed with knobby-jointed fingers—"turn right, and it's on the next corner. Bernie's Beer and Balls. You can't miss it."

"Thank you," she tossed out as she ducked into her car and turned the key.

"You come on back sometime and visit," the older woman called out before turning her attention back to her flowers.

As Lydia neared the end of the street, she cautioned herself to slow down and turn carefully. But she was so worried. Tears were now threatening at the back of her eyes, blurring her vision.

She was pleading with God as she parked and jumped out of the car. Bernie's was hopping, and the parking lot was full. She spotted Andy's truck. Thank God.

Inside, smoke hung like smog, obscuring the view and clogging her lungs. Her eyes burned, making her close them several times before they adjusted. No one seemed to notice her coming in, just moved aside as she made her way toward the bar.

Even over the din of talking, laughter, and music coming from the ancient jukebox, she heard the distinctive cracking sound of billiard balls hitting billiard balls. The pool tables were toward the back.

She moved toward the back, sidestepping waitresses with trays of drinks and happy customers hanging around already-full tables, beer mugs in their hands and laughter in their voices. They were all starting to annoy her.

She stopped, standing on tiptoe to see down the two rows of pool tables. When she spotted Andy leaning against a wall while someone else was bent over the table, she wanted to run to him. She dodged to the right as the player pushed his cue stick out behind his right side before shoving it forward for his shot.

"Andy!" she gushed, grabbing his arm when she arrived at his side.

His head jerked around to look down at her. He registered the panic in her voice and saw it in her eyes.

"What's wrong?" He was instantly alert, taking her by the arm and leading her off to a corner where they could have a little privacy.

"Brandon isn't at home. Do you know where he is?" Her eyes begged him to tell her where her son was, but she could tell by his expression that he didn't know.

"I dropped him off at the usual time and watched until he unlocked the door and went inside. Then I left. Where have you looked?"

As she filled him in on the places she had been, his gut cramped in fear that something had happened to Brandon. Had he been kidnapped?

"All of his friends were at home, and none of them have seen him," she said, her voice cracking on the last words while tears filled her eyes.

"Listen, just calm down," he urged, wrapping an arm around her as he drew her with him. "Mike, I have to leave. Sorry, buddy," he said as he stood his cue stick in the holder mounted on the wall.

"That's all right, man. Looks like you have a much better offer," his friend joked.

They didn't wait around to banter with his buddies, their thoughts already propelling them out into the growing dusk.

"Okay, I think you should go home in case he shows up back there," he instructed, stopping by her car.

"No, I—"

"Shh. Listen, I'll head out to look for him some more. You have my cell phone number, don't you?" He reached into his pocket and pushed a button on the phone. "Okay, it's turned on now." As he opened the car door for her and ushered her inside, he continued. "I'll look for him, and if he shows up at home or if I find him, we'll call each other, agreed?" He could tell that she wasn't happy with the

In Daddy's Shoes

thought of going home and sitting there waiting and not actively doing anything to find her son.

"Okay," she finally agreed, letting out the breath she had been holding while her thoughts were in turmoil.

She rolled down the window and leaned out. "Andy, thank you. I don't know where else to look, and I'm so afraid," she whispered, looking up into his eyes.

He stepped in close to the car, reaching in to squeeze her shoulder. "I'll call every so often while I'm looking for him. Just be brave, and we'll find him. Now, drive carefully," he ordered, stepping back and waiting for her to start the car and put it into gear.

Even before she was out of the parking lot, he was jogging to his truck, his mind already focused on places he could look for the missing boy.

Brandon was cold, but he just huddled closer to the tombstone marking the grave where his father was buried. He didn't remember much about the day of the funeral—it was pretty much a blur—but he remembered that his mother had cried a lot. He remembered people telling them that time would heal the wounds and that he was the man of the house now.

That was the part that had worried him the most. His father had said pretty much the same thing on the last day they saw him before he went overseas to war. He couldn't remember much about that day either, except that his mother had been crying then too and his father had called him his "little man." His father had also told him to take care of everything until he got back home.

OWEN COUNTY PUBLIC LIBRARY

"That's the part I'm having trouble with, Dad. I can't take care of everything. I don't know how. I want to take care of Mom, but I don't know how to do that either. But now there's Mr. Jenkins, and he seems to like Mom." He wiped the tears from his face with one hand while the other was pressed against the cold stone. "He held her hand just like you used to do. I don't know if you'd like that or not. I just don't know," he whispered, bowing his head and allowing the tears to drip into his lap.

"The only problem, Dad, is that the older I get, the more I know I'm not big enough or strong enough to take care of things. That leaves Mom to handle it." His eyes rose to look at his father's name on the gray stone.

"She's doing an all right job, I guess, but I'm not much help. Sometimes I think I get in the way and make more trouble for her. Dad"—he spoke in earnest—"I don't want to make her cry. I'm sorry."

He flinched when he heard leaves crunch behind him. He jerked his head around to see Mr. Jenkins coming toward him. He turned around quickly and wiped his tears away, sliding his hands down the front of his pants to dry them.

"Hi, Brandon." He spoke softly as he sat down on the ground beside the boy. He pulled his knees up toward his chest and linked his hands together around his legs. He sat quietly for a few moments, giving the boy time to adjust to the intrusion.

"You know, your mother is very worried since she came home and you weren't there. She's been looking all over for you." He paused, tilting his head a little to see if Bran-

In Daddy's Shoes

don was listening. "Do you want to use my cell phone to call her and let her know you're all right?"

The boy still had his head down, clenching his hands tightly in his lap. Andy remained quiet and just waited. When Brandon raised his head, there were tears glistening in his eyes.

"Did I make her cry?"

Andy wasn't sure how to answer that question. He didn't want to lie, but he didn't want Brandon to think he had hurt his mother.

"She's just worried about you. If you call her, tell her where you are and that you needed a little time to yourself, I think she'll understand." Again he held his cell phone toward the boy and waited.

After a couple seconds of looking at the object as if it were a snake, the boy slumped a little but reached to take the phone.

After punching in the numbers, he barely had to wait before the call was answered.

"Mom? It's me." His head drooped before he spoke again. "I'm fine. I'm with Mr. Jenkins, and we're over at the cemetery visiting Dad. We'll be home soon," he muttered. After listening for a few moments, he clicked the phone closed and handed it back. Andy allowed the silence to linger. He felt Brandon needed the time.

When Brandon raised his head to look at him, he made the decision to share his story with the boy.

"Did you know that my father was killed when I was twelve?" Andy didn't make it a habit to tell people much about himself, but he knew Brandon needed to know he wasn't the only boy to lose a father. He immediately had Brandon's attention. The boy was instantly alert, moving to get a more direct view of the man beside him. He was looking at the teacher with new interest.

"No. Did he die in a war?"

"No, he died when a drunk driver came over into our lane and slammed into our car, right against his door. My mother and I were injured, but he was the only one to die."

A heavy silence settled on the two as they continued to sit, shoulders almost touching, both staring at the gravestone where Steven Reynolds' name was etched into the cold stone.

"Did you feel like you were supposed to become the man of the house? Did everyone tell you to take care of your mother?"

Andy's heart ached for the boy. He understood the weight that was pressing down on his young shoulders, shoulders too thin to carry the load of an adult.

"For a while, yes. I thought it was my fault if something wasn't going right. I felt responsible if there wasn't enough money in the house to take care of all the bills or for my mother to get a new dress for Easter like she always had before."

There was a long silence before Brandon looked up again into the older man's eyes. "You said you felt that way 'for a while.' How long was that? When did it get better?"

Andy knew he had to be careful how he answered the question. It was a grown-up question that deserved a grown-up answer.

"My father died when I was twelve, and my mother never remarried. He had been gone almost six years when

In Daddy's Shoes 105

I graduated high school, and I delayed college for a couple of years so I could earn some money and pay off my mother's house before starting to go into debt for my education. She always called me her "little man," and I felt responsible for her. I felt I had to provide for her and my little sister since my father wasn't there to do it. I was trying to grow up fast and be the man before I was supposed to be, and I started getting angry at the world. I was even angry with my mother, even though it wasn't her fault."

"Why were you angry with your mother if you were the one to decide to take care of her? She didn't ask you to, did she?" It was getting dark, but a security light near the church cast a dim glow across the cemetery. Brandon had turned to stare at his teacher, searching the man's face.

"I guess I had things mixed up in my head. She didn't expect me to literally be the man of the house or to take care of her, but I felt responsible because so many people called me 'the little man' or 'the man of the house.' I was mistaken to feel that way. I was only a kid, and it was the responsibility of the grown-ups to take care of things." He sat in silence, allowing Brandon to analyze what he had said.

The boy sat silently for several moments, gazing at his hands, before he spoke.

"The last thing my dad said to me before he left was that I was the 'man of the family now' and that it was my responsibility to 'take care of things' until he got home. I wasn't sure what that meant at first, but after he died and Mom cried all the time, I figured it was my job to make sure she wasn't unhappy and didn't cry. I think I messed up again, though," he mumbled, picking at a scab on the back of one finger.

"You mean because you needed a little time to yourself?"

Brandon looked up at the man sitting next to him. The way he put it, it didn't sound so bad. It almost sounded as if the man was talking to another grown-up. Kids ran away or had time outs, but only adults "needed a little time to yourself." A tiny smile lurked at the corner of his lips.

"Yeah."

"Well, it seems to me that needing to be alone is normal enough. The part that needs a little repair is the disappearing without letting your mother know where you were going. She was worried about your safety." He kept his voice low, not wanting to upset the boy further.

"Guess I blew that part. Do you think she'll ground me?"

"I'm not sure, but if you level with her the way you did with me, I think the whole process will go a little easier for you. I can't guarantee anything, but I think she'll understand if you explain," he suggested, standing up and reaching down to hoist the boy to his feet.

"Come on. Let's get you home. You're probably cold and hungry."

"Will you go inside with me?" There was fear in his eyes, and his voice quivered a little as he waited for the answer.

"Yes, I can, but you have to do the talking. In fact, I suggest that you two talk alone, maybe in your bedroom, and then join me for some hot chocolate. How does that sound?"

"Okay," Brandon mumbled, his head hanging low.

Andy thought the boy resembled a prisoner walking to the gas chamber. It was all he could do to keep a smile off his face. After all, this was a very serious time for Brandon. How the adults in his life treated this situation might affect him for a long, long time. He wished he could call

In Daddy's Shoes

and talk with Lydia before they got to the house, but he would just have to trust that she wouldn't fly off the handle. She appeared to be a rational and patient person. He'd have to have faith in her.

It was apparent that Brandon wasn't as confident.

Lydia had been carrying the phone around the house with her ever since she got home and didn't find a message from Brandon. Where could he be? What if something had happened to him?

"No, I won't think that way. Nothing has happened. He's fine. He'll be home soon," she told herself. Her words echoed in the quiet house.

She immediately punched the talk button when the phone in her hand began to ring.

"Mom? It's me."

The sound of Brandon's voice slammed into her like a fist to the stomach. She doubled over to sag onto the couch as she listened to his hesitant yet sweet voice. Every bit of strength drained from her body as she dropped down, her head almost resting on her knees as she pressed the phone to her ear.

"Are you all right?"

"I'm fine. I'm with Mr. Jenkins, and we're over at the cemetery visiting Dad. We'll be home soon."

"Okay. I'll see you when you get here," she told him, clicking the phone off before he could hear the tears in her voice. She didn't want him to know she was crying. She knew it upset him. When Steven died, she had cried all the time, but after a while she noticed how nervous her son got when she broke down. After that she tried to cry only late at night after Brandon was in bed or when she was in the shower or the car alone.

But today was different. For a moment, she had been forced to imagine life without Brandon. She slid to the floor on her knees, leaning over the seat of the sofa and laying her forehead on the cushion as her eyes closed, her heart aching, sending up a prayer of gratitude.

It took several minutes before she had the strength to stand up. She had to wipe her mind clean of the fear and anxiety that had bound her. Her son was on his way home.

Suddenly she thought about Andy. How had he known where to look for Brandon? She never would have thought her son would go to the cemetery alone. It was almost five miles away. She shuddered to think about all the traffic he had ridden his bike through to get there. Thank goodness he was being driven home.

She walked toward the kitchen to hang up the phone, but her mind wasn't cooperating. She stood at the counter and stared blankly at the bowl of fruit on the counter. The bananas were getting a little too ripe. Maybe she'd make banana bread. Brandon loved it, and it was quick and easy.

She laid the phone on the counter and began to get out the ingredients to make the cake. Five minutes later she was sliding the loaf pan into the oven.

Every few minutes she glanced up at the clock. What was taking so long? Were they talking? The thought irritated her at first, but the reality was that she had asked Andy to help her with Brandon, and that was what he was doing. How could she be angry with him? In fact, anger wasn't what came to mind when she thought about Andy.

Far from it. She shook her head, running her hands through her hair. She probably looked a mess.

Soon she was in the bathroom running a brush through her hair, pulling it back into a ponytail. She stood for a moment looking into her own eyes in the mirror. Had her eyes given her away last Sunday? She had sat beside Mr. and Mrs. Ferguson in church, and as soon as she walked outside with them, Arnold Ferguson asked Brandon about school, and the boy had started telling the older man all about his teacher, football, and their recent fishing trip. Emily Ferguson had smiled a knowing smile and winked at Lydia.

"I hear he's eligible, Lydia, and good-looking too. Why don't you introduce yourself or ask him over for dinner?"

She couldn't believe that a woman almost twice her age would suggest that. She herself was old school, expecting the guy to ask the girl for a date, not the other way around.

On second thought, though, maybe she could invite Andy over for dinner to thank him for all he had been doing for Brandon. Yeah, that might work. She could make her famous pot roast with carrots and potatoes. It was one of Brandon's favorite meals and sure to be a hit with Andy.

She caught her thoughts and stopped them. Did she want to impress Andy with her cooking? Did she really want that kind of complication in her life right now when her hands were full with her job and son? Was she even ready to allow another man into her life, or into the life of her son? If she remarried, she would have to deal with the fact that another man would help guide her son into manhood. Was she ready for that?

She shook her head, running her hands under her eyes. "I don't know. I just don't know. I'm just not going to worry about it right now." She sighed before turning back to the kitchen. "I need to get him through fourth grade first," she mumbled. "Then I'll worry about the rest of his life."

Her thoughts turned again to Andy and her dilemma of asking him over for dinner. Should she? Would he think she was too forward?

"Well, it's only polite to do something to thank Andy, and if it leads to a date or two, then that might be fun as well. I just have to keep my eyes open. I'll know when to stop it," she told herself, muttering as she headed back to the kitchen to start a pot of coffee.

She had just checked the banana bread, figuring it had another ten minutes before it would be ready to come out of the oven, when she heard a vehicle drive up out front. The dessert was forgotten as she ran to peek out the front window. Both doors opened, but Andy waited for Brandon to get out before they headed to the front door.

Lydia darted for the kitchen. She didn't want either of them to know that she was anxious. She wanted to appear calm and relaxed so Brandon wouldn't be upset. She had time to take three mugs down from the cupboard. Brandon would probably want hot chocolate while they had coffee.

When the front door opened, she glanced up, giving them a smile. Brandon kept looking at the floor but stopped in the middle of the living room when Andy put a hand on the boy's shoulder.

She set the packet of hot chocolate on the counter and without a word walked to her son to gather him into her arms. His thin arms came up around her waist, squeezing

In Daddy's Shoes

tightly as she drew him near and hugged his trembling body close.

"I'm sorry, Mom. I didn't mean to upset you," he said, leaning away to look up into her face. "I needed to talk with Dad, that's all."

"It's okay, honey, but next time please let me know so I don't worry about you." He nodded his head, wiping his eyes quickly.

"Why don't you go in and wash up, and I'll make you a sandwich? Then you can have some dessert," she suggested. "Scoot," she said, smiling gently as she stepped back.

Andy watched her staring after Brandon as the boy turned and left the room, his head still hung down, his shoulders still slumped forward.

When she turned to face Andy, her eyes reflected the pain and anguish that had been ripping her apart. He wasn't even aware of moving toward her until he had pulled her into his arms. It felt right. She felt good in his arms. Was this what he had been missing? A woman who had a tender heart? A woman who would love her children more than herself? Would she love her man with the same intensity? Somehow he was sure that she would.

Her head was tucked under his chin, his broad hands rubbing her back while his mind raged on. This felt so good, this warm body snuggled up to him, depending on him. *Depending on him?* That thought made his breathing jerk and his muscles tighten. Was she depending on him? Is that what he wanted in his life right now? He'd have to think about that . . . later.

He released his hold when she gently pushed back from his warmth. She had felt him stiffen. She had felt the change in the hold he had on her that she had needed, even craved, with every fiber of her body. She had missed the touches, the caresses, and the reassuring closeness she and Steven had enjoyed while he was alive. But was it Steven she missed now or just the physical touch?

"Mom?"

At the sound of her son's voice behind her, she jumped like a teenager whose father had just caught her necking with her boyfriend. She stepped back, pulling out of the loose touch Andy had maintained on her and plastered a smile onto her face as she turned to face her son.

"Yes, honey?"

"Is everything okay?" His eyes were scouring her face, looking deeply into her eyes.

Her smile broadened. "Yes, everything is fine. I was just thanking Andy for finding you and bringing you home." She rubbed her damp palms down the front of her slacks before turning to head toward the kitchen, tossing her offer over her shoulder.

"I had been planning to make hamburgers for dinner. Is anyone hungry?"

Andy looked at the boy to see how he was reacting to finding his mother in the arms of a man who wasn't his father. Brandon was staring at him, his face blank for several seconds before he shrugged and headed for the kitchen.

"I'm hungry. Do we have chips?"

Chapter Ten

It had been a week since Lydia had tracked him to the pub and he had found Brandon at his father's grave. The situation ran through his mind like a news release on a loop. It was never far from his mind.

When he was away from Lydia for a few days, he felt that he didn't want anyone in his life to mess up the routine he had established after he and Sheryl split. He liked Lydia, but why mess up a good thing? He had the perfect life now. Right? He had his work, which he loved, he had a home that was neat and clean, and he had peace and quiet. He could relax with a ball game and a beer, and no one would interrupt him. Perfect.

The last thing he had wanted or needed was for his interfering little sister to arrive in town and spend three days trying to convince him to settle down and get married. It had been one argument after another about his allowing his ex-wife to ruin his opinion of women. He had remained adamant that he was happy with his life the way it was, and

Marisa had finally gotten the message. Or at least he hoped she had. He mentally replayed their conversation from their recent dinner together.

"How can you be happy all alone?" Marisa had asked, returning her coffee cup to the table and leaning forward slightly as she continued. "Doesn't the house ever close in on you?" Her eyebrows were drawn together as she tried to understand how he could be content to have no one to come home to and no one to share his day with every evening.

"I'm not always alone, and when I am," he explained, "I'm busy grading papers and things like that. I keep busy." He would never admit that he had suggested eating out because his house was, indeed, closing in on him. He had needed to get out and be around noise and people.

He caught a movement over his sister's shoulder as a woman with a blond ponytail turned to leave through the restaurant. He started to rise to his feet before he realized that he was now seeing Lydia in every blond. He relaxed back into the chair, wrapping his hands around the mug before dragging his eyes back to Marisa's.

"Look, sis, I'm seeing someone, but right now I don't know how serious it is. I like her very much, but I don't want to rush things—you know what I mean?" His eyes beseeched her to drop the subject.

"Oh, really?" Her shoulders relaxed as she smiled. "I'm glad to hear it. In fact, maybe I'll get a chance to meet her the next time I'm in town."

When he had dropped Marisa at the airport, he had been glad to see her leave. If it hadn't been for his sister, he might not have married Sheryl in the first place, and he certainly wasn't going to rush into a relationship and make the same mistake twice. Just as he had taught Brandon on their fishing trip, sometimes you had no choice but to cut bait and move on. Until he could decide just how serious he felt about Lydia, he'd keep things friendly, nothing more.

It was Friday evening, and he had just gotten home from Bernie's pub. He sat on the sofa with the television on mute, just staring at the images flashing on the screen while the local news told about the latest robberies and murders.

Was this all there was to life? Was this how it was supposed to be? Work five days a week, play pool or have a beer with the guys on Friday nights, work in the yard on Saturday, and go to church on Sunday?

As the news anchor told the latest story, Andy stood to pace the floor. He had been unable to get Lydia and Brandon out of his mind. They were always popping up. He looked for her each day at football practice, but she hadn't shown up this week. He had taken Brandon home the afternoon before meeting his sister for dinner at the restaurant, but he hadn't gone inside. Instead, he had waved to the boy and driven off. Cowardly? Yeah, maybe. He hadn't minded that she came to him in an emergency, but he wasn't sure he wanted her to start depending on him all the time.

Maybe he should give her a call and just check on things. Just a few minutes . . . *Hi, how are you? Good? Great! Catch you later.*

Even as he made up his mind and reached for the phone, he knew what he really wanted was to hear her voice. Lydia had a gentle way of speaking that made him think of soft hands gliding over his back, bringing relaxation and pleasure. Her words flowed through his brain right through to his body's core, bringing his thoughts to focus on one woman. Not just any woman but the one woman who had been able to catch and hold his attention since his disastrous marriage. The woman he wished was sitting beside him right now on the sofa.

His palms were slightly damp as he punched in her number.

The phone rang only twice before she picked it up.

"Hello?"

His stomach tightened. This woman could be dangerous to his peace of mind and he was inviting her into his life, but what else could he do? She had already moved into his mind and made herself at home.

"Um, hi. This is Andy," he told her. *You idiot,* he told himself, *she knows who you are.* "I was just wondering how you are. I haven't seen you at the football field all week and wondered if everything is going all right for you," he rushed on to say. Tiny droplets of sweat were popping out at his hairline.

There was a long silence after he stopped talking. Was she still there? Why wasn't she talking to him?

"Are you there?"

"Yes, I'm here. Excuse me a moment," she told him. "I have to turn down the television."

Within moments she was back on the phone, but during those moments his thoughts pummeled him. Was he doing the right thing? Yes, this was right.

"Okay, I'm here."

For a moment he listened to her breathing, his eyes closed as he envisioned her sitting on her sofa. He wished he were there with her.

In Daddy's Shoes

"Um." He cleared his throat as he slid farther down on his spine and put his feet up on the coffee table. "I haven't talked with you much this week, and I've missed it . . . talking with you."

When only silence met his admission, he quickly continued.

"I just got home a little while ago and wanted to call, uh, and see if Brandon would like to do something on Sunday afternoon," he finished up in a rush. What if she said no? Then what?

Her voice floated over the wire to flood him with hope. He could almost smell the perfume that he now associated with her.

"I know Brandon would love it. What do you have in mind?"

He was glad Brandon would enjoy it, but what about Lydia?

"I thought maybe lunch and the new Disney movie that just came out."

"Oh, he'll love that. He's already been asking if we could go. Um, what time did you want him ready?"

The silence hung for a couple of moments before her words registered.

"Are you saying that you don't want to go out with me, uh, I mean, with us?"

"I wasn't sure I was invited. I thought this might be some 'guy time' with Brandon."

What was wrong with her? "Of course you're invited. Why wouldn't you be?" He hated that his frustration was evident in his voice, but he didn't understand what had gotten into her. Why her change of attitude?

"Well, let's see. Maybe it's because you've got a new woman in your life? I didn't want to interfere." Her voice had softened.

"What woman? What are you talking about?" He hated that he was getting angry, but this was going too far. What was she accusing him of? "Wait. Wait just a doggone minute." Was she still hung up about that one date with Connie?

"It's none of my business who you go out with."

"Stop it. Stop it right now," he ordered. He had heard enough. Irritation dripped from every word, but he needed to see her face, her eyes. This wasn't a conversation to have over the phone. "I'm coming over so we can get to the bottom of this."

"No, that's not a good idea. You sound angry, and I don't want that in front of Brandon. If you still want to take him to the movies, I'll have him ready, but I think we've said enough. Good night."

Andy stood holding the receiver to his ear for several seconds after he heard the click on the other end of the wire.

Still he held the phone, extending it out to stare at it for several seconds before slamming it down. He whirled around and kicked a wall. When he saw the hole in the drywall, he was even angrier, but this time it was at himself for losing control.

Lydia pushed the end button down with one finger as she cradled the phone near her chest and sank into the chair. Tears pooled in her eyes. It was over. Before it had even begun. She had pushed him away, and now there was no chance of there ever being a relationship. Still, she refused to be the one he called when he didn't have anyone else to go places with.

She sucked in her breath as she realized that she might ruin Brandon's chance to have Andy as a friend and mentor. No, she was sure that Andy would still see Brandon. She was sure he wouldn't hurt a child. He might like to dangle several women at one time, like Connie and like the woman she'd seen him leaving a restaurant with recently, but he was loyal to the children in his class. She had seen him in action with them. They all loved him, girls and boys alike, and children could spot a phony a mile away.

Her heart was almost breaking as she replaced the phone and stood. Several moments later she was still standing in the same spot, her feet rooted to the carpet as her mind whirled. Had she made a mistake? Had she handled this the right way? But what else could she have said? She had seen him leave with yet another woman. Her eyes didn't lie.

"I won't be a stand-in for some other woman," she declared in a defiant whisper. Her eyes narrowed, and her fists clenched as she thought about him calling to casually ask them to a movie. Had someone else turned him down, so he had a free afternoon? Were she and Brandon an afterthought? Were they a fill-in for an empty slot on his calendar?

Lydia blinked, bringing her wandering, floundering thoughts back to the present. No, she had a hard time imagining Andy being that self-centered. And the more she thought about it, she realized that she had no right to be upset with Andy. He was doing exactly what she had asked him to do; he was helping Brandon over a rough spot in his life. Period.

She pushed stray hairs off her forehead as she mentally shook off the depression that was threatening to close in on her. Her priorities were set. She was first and foremost a mother, and despite her growing feelings for Andy, her son had to come first. Besides, she didn't want to be anyone's second choice. If she couldn't be number one in someone's life, then she'd rather be alone.

Her steps were slow and heavy as she turned down the hall, switching off the light.

Brandon slipped quietly out of the dark bathroom, hesitating only long enough for his mother's bedroom door to close before he tiptoed across the hall to his room. He couldn't believe it. Mr. Jenkins had made his mother cry. He wasn't sure what to think. One day he was holding her hand, and the next day he said something to make her cry. What had he said to her? Did this mean that Mr. Jenkins wouldn't help him with football anymore?

As he thought about what he might lose, he suddenly remembered his father. He remembered how his mom had cried when *he* died. He hated it when his mother cried.

Silently he slipped back into the hallway, making his way down to his mother's bedroom door. No light shone under the door, but still he stepped close and put his ear against the wood. The sound was muffled, but she was crying. As his small fists clenched at his sides, he vowed to make Mr. Jenkins pay for hurting his mom. He wasn't sure how, but the man would have to answer to him . . . and soon.

Chapter Eleven

It was Monday morning, and Brandon was quiet, sullen as he ate his Cheerios and drank his juice. He had said he hadn't felt well, so they hadn't gone to the movies with Andy over the weekend. Now, as she watched him with one elbow on the table, his head propped on his fist, Lydia was worried that he might be coming down with the flu—for real this time.

"Your bus will be here in a few minutes," she reminded him, pressing the back of her hand against the side of his face and his forehead. As usual, he pulled away from her hand but not before she registered that his temperature felt normal.

"Honey, are you worried about a test today or something?" She slid into the chair next to his and picked up her coffee cup, making an effort to appear concerned but not pushy.

"No, and will you just leave me alone? I'm fine," he said, standing up and turning to leave. "I'm fine," he repeated emphatically over his shoulder.

Her first instinct was to order him to stop, to not walk out on the conversation, but she held herself back when she saw how tense his posture was as he stormed out of the room. What was going on? What had him so upset?

Her heart sank a little lower as she sighed, standing to take the dishes to the sink. Couldn't things go right for at least a few weeks in a row? "And he isn't even a teenager yet," she mumbled to herself as she automatically rinsed the dishes and put them into the dishwasher.

If things were on their usual footing, she would have picked up the phone and called Brandon's teacher to ask if something had happened in class or on the football field, but she didn't feel comfortable doing that right now.

Again she wondered if she should have been so curt with Andy the prior Friday night. She had called early on Saturday to tell him that Brandon was sick and had been relieved when he didn't answer, allowing her to just leave a message on his phone.

"Well," she told herself, "if Brandon isn't in a better mood tonight, I'll call Andy. I can't ignore whatever's bothering him or allow him to continue to be rude."

With that decision made, she headed to her bedroom to get ready for work. Her problems with Brandon would have to wait until that evening. Monday was always rough at work, and it was going to be tough enough just making it through the day.

Andy had arrived at school early. As he sat drinking his latte, his mind rehashed what Lydia had said Friday night. Had she been referring to his taking Connie out to dinner?

In Daddy's Shoes

That had been so long ago. Surely she wasn't holding a grudge about one dinner with another woman when he and Lydia had barely met yet.

He leaned his elbows on the desk and propped his chin in the palm of one hand. The fingers of his other hand fiddled with a paper clip in frustration. "I don't understand women. Whoever said they're a mystery hit the nail on the head," he muttered, tossing the paper clip away and beginning to drum his fingers on the scarred desktop.

As he tilted the cup to drain the last of the warm drink, he noticed Brandon standing in the doorway, glaring at him. He slowly brought the cup down and set it on the desk before speaking.

"Good morning, Brandon. Come on in. Did you want to talk with me before class starts?" He glanced at his watch and saw that he had about ten minutes before the other students would start arriving.

Brandon remained sullen but moved into the room and stopped at Andy's desk. Andy saw a storm of emotions in the eyes that bore into his, but he couldn't imagine what had upset the boy to such an extent.

"What's up, son?"

"I'm not your son, and you're not my father," he spat out like a snake striking its prey. "Don't call me your son," he hissed. "My name is Brandon."

Brandon's anger, held barely under control, shocked Andy, slamming into him like an arrow to the heart. He had thought he and Brandon were building a solid relationship, but something was dreadfully wrong, and he knew he had to get to the bottom of whatever had the boy so upset.

"Okay, Brandon. Obviously you're very upset, so why don't you tell me what's on your mind, and we'll see if there's any way I can help you."

Without skipping a heartbeat, the boy's next words spewed forth.

"The only way you can help me is to stay away from my mother. I don't want her hurt anymore. I don't want her to cry anymore. I don't . . ." Silence fell between them while Brandon swallowed a couple of times, blinking to keep the tears from falling.

Andy was instantly on his feet, reaching toward the hurting boy even as Brandon stumbled back to stay beyond the teacher's hand.

Andy instantly stopped when Brandon jerked backward. "Brandon, I'm not going to hurt you. Why don't you sit down," he suggested, indicating the front desk, "and we'll talk this out."

Long moments passed before the boy, wary and with fists still clenched, eased over to the chair and slid into the seat.

"Your outburst and your demand have come as a complete surprise to me, so I'm not sure where to start this conversation." He grabbed the back of his rolling chair and slid it around until he was sitting only a few feet away but level with Brandon.

When Brandon remained silent, Andy took a slow breath, searching for the right words to say.

"Let me start by saying that I would never intentionally hurt you or your mother." When Brandon sucked in a breath, ready to hurl more words at him, Andy's hand shot up in a gesture his students knew well. He was demanding silence.

In Daddy's Shoes

"Please let me finish, and then you can have your turn and respond to what I've said, okay?" When the boy closed his mouth and slid down into the seat with his legs splayed out and his fingers drumming on the desk, Andy continued.

"As I was saying, I would never *intentionally* hurt either of you, but I know that sometimes there can be misunderstandings, and people's feelings can get hurt." He took a slow breath before continuing, fearing that he might be opening a Pandora's box but not knowing how to settle this issue without inviting Brandon to vent his anger.

"Does this have something to do with the telephone conversation I had with your mom last Friday?"

Instantly Brandon pushed himself up into a straight position, his hands flat on the desktop as he glared at his teacher.

"You know it does. You know you said something to her that made her cry, and you don't care. You don't care about either of us. I know—"

He abruptly stopped speaking, his small chest rising and falling rapidly as his anger pumped through him.

"What do you know? Were you listening on another phone in the house?"

"No."

Regardless of his negative answer, the guilt on his face told Andy that Brandon wasn't being totally honest with him.

Andy allowed the silence to stretch, watching emotions flit across the young face, one after another, as the child tried to gather his thoughts and fight for his mother. Andy's chest swelled with the respect he was feeling for the boy. Brandon was only ten, yet he had taken on his teacher in defense of his mother. He was proud of the boy, even if this wasn't the right moment to tell him that.

"Okay, please tell me what has upset you, so we can talk about it," he suggested mildly again, sitting forward and balancing his elbows on his thighs as he loosely intertwined his fingers and allowed them to dangle between his knees.

"You made my mother cry. I don't like that," Brandon mumbled, his eyebrows drawn together over eyes currently focused on the edge of the desk where Brandon was tracing his finger along a groove.

Had Lydia really cried after their last conversation? Why?

"Your mother and I had a grown-up conversation on the phone, and I believe there was a misunderstanding, but since it was too late to come over and talk about it, like you and I are doing now, we hung up. I plan to call her later today to see if we can talk about it and straighten everything out."

Brandon's eyes rose to meet his teacher's steady gaze. Andy sensed that the storm had passed, but every word he said and everything he did would be weighed and measured against a ten-year-old boy's perspective of adult relationships.

He glanced at his watch again before speaking. He still had a few minutes, if he was lucky. "While I've got a few minutes alone with you, I'd like to ask you a question." He knew he was taking a chance, but he needed to ask Brandon how he felt.

Brandon was silent, but he was looking the older man right in the eye, meeting him stare for stare. Andy's pride in the boy took another step higher. Brandon was giving every impression of being more mature than his years. Well, he could certainly understand having to grow up in a hurry when life dealt you a rough set of cards.

"Okay, here's the deal. You know I like you, right?" He waited until he saw Brandon's chin move a fraction of an inch. "Well, I also like your mother, and I'd like to date her—you know, get to know her better." He waited, but the boy's eyes didn't falter or give any indication of his inner feelings.

"If you don't have any major objections, I'd like to ask her out for dinner now and then, but I want you to understand that I will never—I repeat, never—intentionally hurt your mother. I will do my best never to make her cry." He could understand that part of Brandon's upset as well, since he had hated it when his mother was thinking about his father and couldn't control her emotions. Yes, he understood.

Brandon sat staring at his teacher as if he was sizing him up. His eyes had narrowed slightly, and his index finger was tapping lightly on the desktop.

"You promise?"

Andy's heart leaped. The boy was going to trust him. At least he was going to give him a chance to prove himself. "Yes, I promise." Andy stuck his hand out, waiting for Brandon to decide whether or not to shake on their agreement. Andy's heart's rhythm kicked up a notch while he waited, unsure how the child would react. When the boy's hand rose to take the larger one in solemn agreement, Andy's heart soared. He felt tears threatening behind his eyes, but he blinked several times as he smiled.

"Okay," the boy agreed softly.

"Don't worry anymore, okay? I'll call your mom this afternoon after school and get everything straightened out. For now, though, why don't you get your books from your locker so you won't be late when the bell rings in a couple of minutes," he said, standing and placing a hand on the boy's shoulder and giving it a light squeeze.

He watched Brandon leave, his head down as he stared at the toes of his tennis shoes. The boy reminded him so much of himself that it was like watching a movie of his own youth—not knowing whom to trust and being afraid the important adults in your life would leave or die like his father had. Yes, he understood what was running through Brandon's mind. Knowing didn't make it a whole lot easier to help him through it, though.

As the bell rang, the noise level in the hallways and classrooms increased to a laughing, yelling, pounding beat that didn't decrease until the second bell rang and everyone was in their seats.

It was going to be a long day until he could talk with Lydia, but at least Brandon wouldn't be glaring at him anymore. Things could be a lot worse.

Chapter Twelve

Brandon wasn't sure if he could trust Mr. Jenkins, but he sure wanted to. It had been cool having someone to play ball with and go places with and fish with. Also he could talk with Mr. Jenkins about stuff that his mother wouldn't understand, like being afraid at first of playing football. His mother might have made him quit the team if he had told her about being nervous about catching a pass, since the other guys would then be trying to slam him to the ground.

All the other guys had their dads in the stands cheering for them, but now he had Mr. Jenkins. He was cool with that. Even if Mr. Jenkins yelled for some of the other kids, he still yelled the most for him. The thought made him smile as he walked from the gym locker room.

Tomorrow was their first real game, and he had to take his uniform home to be washed. He hoped his mother sat with Mr. Jenkins. It would sort of be like having a mother and father at the game.

He was smiling as he rounded the corner of the building

and saw his mother waiting for him in the car. He glanced around, but he didn't see Mr. Jenkins' truck. Had he already left?

"Hi, honey," his mother called out.

Jeez, it was embarrassing to have your mother call you "honey." He glanced around and was relieved to see that none of the guys was close enough to hear.

He jerked open the back door, tossing the uniform inside.

"How was your day?" his mom asked cheerfully.

"Where's Mr. Jenkins?" he asked in return, still searching the parking lot in case he had missed him.

"I'm not sure, but I got a message at work that he wouldn't be able to take you home today, so I'm here," she said, smiling over at her son, who was now slouching down in the seat, his lips compressed into a thin line.

"Hey, it's not the end of the world, you know. I thought we'd stop for Chinese food and then rent a movie. How about that?"

"Yeah, I guess it's okay," he grumbled, crossing his arms and turning his face toward the window.

Lydia wasn't sure what was going through her son's mind, but maybe she'd call Andy later and see if he had any clue. If she knew what was on Brandon's mind, she might be able to help him. In the meantime, she'd try not to pressure him and stay as upbeat as possible.

The evening had disintegrated, with Brandon's surly attitude ruining the meal and the movie before Lydia gave up and sent him to bed. It was obvious he was upset about something, yet he denied it whenever she asked him.

In Daddy's Shoes

She poured herself a glass of wine to give her the nerve to pick up the phone and call Andy.

On the second ring a female answered.

"Hello?"

"Oh, I'm sorry. I was . . . I wanted . . . Never mind, I'll call back later," she stammered.

"Andy will be back shortly. Can I have him call you?"

"No, thanks," she mumbled, replacing the phone. She sat staring at the amber glass of wine sitting on the coffee table. Was this the same woman she had seen him with a few days ago? Or was it a new one? Her heart felt like breaking, but she refused to cry. She had to keep her focus on helping Brandon, even if it hurt to discover that what she was beginning to feel toward Andy was one-sided.

She stood to walk aimlessly around the room, touching books on the shelf and candleholders on the mantel. When she got to a framed photograph of her husband, she touched the picture, sliding her finger down one side of his face.

"I miss having an adult to talk with," she told the picture. "I miss having someone to help me figure out what our son is going through."

The phone's jarring ring interrupted her musing. She was able to get to it before it rang a second time.

"Hello?"

"Lydia? It's Andy. Did you just call here?"

"Yes, but . . . it's not important. You're busy, so don't worry about it," she told him, trying her best to keep her voice calm.

"I'm not doing anything special. What did you want?"

"Nothing special?" She was confused. "I think your 'friend' might disagree with you. I'll talk with you another time. Good night." Her voice had dropped to almost a whisper by the time she hung up the phone.

She was embarrassed that she had interrupted him with another woman. She was also disgusted with herself for not being strong enough to tell him why she had called and to ask her questions. Why had she hung up? How was she going to be able to face him at Brandon's games or, heaven forbid, at the next parent-teacher conference? She shuddered just thinking about it.

Andy stood with the phone in his hand for several moments after hearing the click on the other end. He couldn't believe she had just hung up on him, when she was the one who had called him in the first place. What was wrong with her?

"Is something the matter?" Marisa took a swallow of her soda while she waited for his answer.

"Huh? Uh, I don't know."

"Who was on the phone?"

"It's a woman I've been . . . seeing for a while. She just hung up without telling me why she had called earlier. Strange," he said, hanging up the phone and frowning as he shook his head. "I'm confused. I guess I'll never understand women," he admitted, mustering a tiny chuckle.

"Let me ask you a question." When he turned to look at her, she continued. "Does she know I'm visiting?"

"Sure . . . well, no, maybe not. I don't think I mentioned it, because you called at the last minute about your plane's layover, and I've hardly spoken to her since. In fact, I had to leave a message with a secretary today telling her I wouldn't be at the football field this afternoon and to be sure that she would be there to take her son home after practice."

"Her son? Is she divorced?"

"Widowed. About two years now," he said, picking up the television remote.

Silence fell like a shroud for several moments before Marisa burst out laughing.

"You are such a dope." She laughed. "Hey, buddy, don't frown at me. You're the one who's dense."

"Okay, okay. Spit it out. What's so funny?"

"Think about it from her point of view for a moment. She hasn't heard from you in a while, and then you call to cancel driving her son home after practice."

The realization of where she was going with the conversation slammed into Andy like a fist to the stomach. "And then when she calls here, a woman answers," he finished for her.

"Right! Okay, so you're not too dense, just a dope," she said, still laughing. "If you care about the woman, call her back." When Andy didn't move, she threw a pillow at him, smacking him in the chest. "Now," she ordered.

He grabbed the phone and headed into his bedroom to make the call, dialing on his way.

Lydia had just set the alarm system and turned off the hall light when the phone rang again. She was sure it was Andy, but she wasn't in the mood to talk with him. She just wanted to be left alone. For one moment she even considered letting it keep ringing, but she didn't want it to wake Brandon. Darting toward the table, she was able to grab it before it rang again.

"Hello?"

"Lydia, it's Andy."

"Why . . . why are you calling?"

"I think we've had a misunderstanding."

"Oh? I'm not aware of any misunderstanding between us. I think we should call it a night, though. It's getting kind of late."

"Wait! Wait! Lydia?"

"Yes," she said slowly, "I'm still here."

"Can you let me explain? I think you misunderstood . . ."

"Andy, it's getting late," she repeated "and I have to go."

"Would you listen to me?" He was almost shouting but paused to take a deep breath before continuing. He counted it a miracle that she hadn't already hung up the phone.

Instantly his decision was made.

"I'm coming over. This isn't a conversation for over the telephone." Before she could come up with any excuses, he slammed the phone down, grabbed his jacket from the closet near the front door, and stormed out. He counted it as a good omen that the phone didn't immediately start ringing after he hung up.

In less than twenty minutes Andy was parking in Lydia's driveway. He shuddered to think about all the yellow lights he had scooted through, but he hadn't been in the mood to sit idling at a stoplight.

Even before he had mounted the few steps leading up to the front door, it swung inward on silent hinges.

Andy stopped when he got to the porch, staring at the vision framed in the doorway. Her hair was down around her shoulders, with a glow behind her from a living room

In Daddy's Shoes

lamp. He propelled himself forward, stretching out his arms as he got near.

As he guided her backward into the foyer, he used one foot to bump the door shut even as he pulled her close, lifting his hands from her shoulders to gently cup her face. Her eyes had never left his as he moved in closer, and as she lifted her chin to maintain eye contact, her lips parted. Without waiting for permission, he swooped in to capture her lips, inhaling her fragrance as he lifted her up onto her toes.

Lydia was startled for a moment at how swiftly Andy had changed their relationship. She felt overwhelmed and invaded yet cherished and loved. He was a big man, but he was gentle. His lips pressed against hers, staking his claim as his fingers slid up into her hair, pushing it away from her face.

Suddenly the memory of a female answering his phone flooded her mind. She tensed as she pushed against his chest, putting some distance between them.

Lydia's troubled eyes looked up into his, begging him to calm her fears and make everything all right. He leaned his forehead in to rest against hers as he closed his eyes to savor the moment.

"I wasn't sure how you'd react when I got here, but at least you didn't call me back right away to tell me not to come," he said, kissing the tip of her nose. Her hand was cold when he reached down, grasping it to lead her toward the sofa. He didn't want to break the physical contact. He needed to touch her.

"Andy, I'm not sure this is a good thing," she started hesitantly.

"Please give me a moment to explain, and I think I can clear up this misunderstanding." Andy sat on the sofa while Lydia perched on the edge of a chair. He leaned in, using one finger to lift her chin until she was looking at him.

"First of all, let me explain about the woman who answered my phone. Marisa is my younger sister." He saw the momentary doubt in Lydia's eyes, but he squeezed her fingers, willing her to listen and believe him.

"She's a pilot for United Airlines and just popped in for a few days before she has to fly out again. She lives in Denver and, due to a mix-up in their plane scheduling, she had a few extra days before her next flight. Normally they would have flown her back to Denver, but she decided to use the time to visit."

Andy was unable to read her eyes. What was she thinking? Did she believe him? He wanted to plead or beg her to accept his explanation, but he wanted her to come to the conclusion that she could trust him on her own, and he was willing to give her time to think through everything he had ever told her about himself. He wouldn't push her for an instant decision—even though that was what he wanted.

The moments dragged by as he watched her eyes, looking for even a hint of what must be going on in her mind. When she frowned slightly, his hopes dropped to his feet.

"So if I call your home number right now, this woman, Marisa, will answer?"

"Yes."

"And if I ask her if she's your sister, she'll say yes to that also?"

"Yes. There are times when she thinks I'm a dope, and I think she even called me 'dense,' but I think she'll still claim

In Daddy's Shoes

me as her brother," he said, risking a grin in hopes of lightening the mood.

He watched her shoulders relax, slumping as she released his hand and slid back into the chair. Her eyes closed for a moment before popping open to glare at him from under a puckered brow.

"Why didn't you tell me before?"

He smiled as his hands came up to playfully hold off any darts she might shoot at him. "Guilty as charged. I'm really sorry. I've had so much on my mind, and I was enjoying catching up on all the news from Colorado, and before I realized it, it was too late last night to call you."

"Well," she said, standing and wiping her palms down the legs of her jeans, "I'm glad that's settled. Uh, do you want a cup of coffee or something?" She had already turned toward the kitchen when Andy grabbed her hand and twirled her around.

"Come here," he instructed her softly. "I've missed you," he said, leaning in to lightly brush his lips across hers. "I'm glad you didn't tell me not to come over," he continued, nuzzling her neck as he worked his way back up to her mouth.

When she could speak again, she smiled up into his eyes.

"I wasn't sure what to say. I wasn't really given a chance to say anything before you hung up on me. Actually . . ." she said, allowing him to sit down first and then sitting close to snuggle against his chest. When his arm wrapped around her shoulders, she continued. "I started to call you back, but then I realized that I wanted you to come over, so I hung the phone up and just waited."

He couldn't believe that she was finally in his arms. Her

words penetrated, slowing his heart rate. There was hope for him with Lydia and her son. His future was looking brighter. He had figured to grow old alone after Sheryl, but suddenly the thought of tomorrow and all the tomorrows after that made him laugh out loud as he squeezed Lydia's shoulders.

Lydia's arms shyly crept up around his neck, but soon she was leaning in to kiss her way up his neck, across his jaw, and finally to his lips.

Brandon crept back to his room and silently closed the door. Toby was right. Mr. Jenkins wanted his mother. They were sneaking around and kissing after they thought he was asleep. "I wonder how long that's been going on," he questioned the darkness as he flopped on to the bed. A small fist slammed into his pillow. Toby was right.

Chapter Thirteen

Lydia was up early the next day, humming while she mixed pancake batter for Brandon's favorite breakfast.

Andy had only stayed until eleven o'clock, but she had lain awake for hours after he kissed her at the door and then drove away into the night. There had been no direct words of love or long-term commitment, just words about caring and admissions to each other that they were interested in pursuing a relationship. They wanted to get to know each other better, and they agreed that the relationship would be exclusive unless they both agreed to break it off.

When she had showered and gotten into bed, the song "Tomorrow" from the movie *Annie* had run over and over through her mind. Tomorrow was her new future, and she couldn't wait for it to arrive. Suddenly her world looked rosy and full of promise.

She was doing a little two-step to the music in her head when the phone rang. A smile splashed across her face. Maybe it was Andy.

"Hello," she said as she leaned her elbows on the counter, resting the phone against her ear.

"Hi, Lydia, this is Marian."

The woman's voice was like a cold breeze across Lydia's skin. She had never been particularly close with her former mother-in-law, but for Brandon's sake she tried to be pleasant whenever the woman called or visited.

"Oh, hi. I'm afraid that Brandon isn't up yet. Can I have him call you later?"

"No. The fact of the matter is that I want to speak with you."

Lydia couldn't imagine anything the woman would want to talk with her about, but she was sure it was either that she wanted her grandson to spend a weekend or she had come up with something else she wanted to criticize about how Lydia was raising Brandon.

"Oh? What's that?"

"I called and spoke with my grandson recently, and he told me that he's playing football."

Oh, so that was going to be her gripe today.

"Yes, he is, and he's doing very well at it. The coach says he's a natural-born athlete."

"Well, I think he's a little young for that rough a sport, but I guess there's nothing I can do about that now. The real reason I called was that he kept talking about a Mr. Jenkins. The man was mentioned in almost every breath. You would think the man walked on water or something." Without waiting for Lydia to take a breath, she continued.

"Anyway, I just wanted you to know about it so you can nip it in the bud before he gets too involved with the man.

Of course, I'm sure he's very nice, but he's not Brandon's father, so he needs to learn the boundaries."

Lydia was stunned. Who did this woman think she was to just call up and act as if it was up to her whom Brandon could spend time with? Lydia took several deep breaths in an effort to calm down before reacting to the woman's outrageous statements.

"First of all, Marian, Mr. Jenkins is Brandon's fourth-grade teacher, and he *is* a very nice man."

"Oh, I'm sure he is. I wasn't saying he's a pedophile or anything. Besides, they run checks on teachers nowadays. But I still think he must be spending too much time with Brandon."

"Well, don't worry about how much time Brandon spends with Andy, because I approve. In fact, I've asked him to get more involved in my son's life, and I'm quite pleased with the way things are going." There, that was telling her.

There was a lengthy silence before Marian's outrage blurted over the phone.

"'Andy'? Are you telling me that you're involved with this teacher? Are you subjecting my grandson to his influence? Are you . . . are you having an affair with the man?" Her disgust was obvious; her voice dripped with loathing as she implied that there was something immoral or illicit going on in front of the child.

Lydia was shocked that her former mother-in-law would ask such a personal question and imply with her tone that she thought inappropriate things were going on in front of Brandon. How dare she? Even though she felt the answer was none of the older woman's business, there was no way she would allow the woman's fertile imagination to harbor such thoughts.

"Personally, I don't think it's any of your business, but the answer to your question is no. I'm not having an affair. However, we are pursuing a relationship, getting to know each other, and I think it's a good thing for me as well as for Brandon."

"How can you say that? How can you say that it's a good thing for Brandon to get attached to another man?"

"Brandon needs a male influence in his life, and since his father is dead, it's time for me to consider allowing another man in to give Brandon the mentoring he needs to grow into a decent person."

The click resounded loudly in Lydia's ear.

"Interfering old biddy," she mumbled, slamming the phone down. "Can't she see that two years without a father has been hard on her grandson?" She sagged down onto a kitchen stool, wrapping her trembling hands around her coffee mug and staring out the window into the backyard. "And hard on me," she whispered.

Once she was calmer, it was easier to give more thought to Marian's feelings. Steven had been her only child, and she had lost him. It must have been excruciating for her. Maybe the woman was just afraid that if Brandon had a stepfather, he'd forget his real father. Didn't Marian know that Lydia would never allow that to happen?

She sighed as she stood to refill her mug before she had to wake Brandon. She smiled as she remembered how reluctant Andy had seemed when it came time for him to leave the evening before. He never suggested staying overnight, which she wouldn't have allowed anyway, but her heart pounded just thinking about the man's kisses.

She rolled her eyes as she swirled around in a circle before wrapping her arms around herself. Was she in love again? It sure felt like it.

Chapter Fourteen

Their movie and lunch outing was a disaster. Brandon slouched in his seat, pouting through the film and only grunting answers when asked about it during lunch.

When Andy offered him four quarters, Brandon took the money without saying a word and disappeared into the game room of the family restaurant.

"What in the world is wrong with him today?" From the moment she had greeted him that morning with her usual, "Good morning, Sunshine," he had been grumpy. He had slumped in the kitchen chair, shoving bites of food into his mouth without saying a word. When she had reminded him about the movie and lunch, he had just shrugged.

She took a few moments to tell Andy about her morning with Brandon, and then she spread her hands out, palms up, as she shrugged. "What can I do? I don't even know what's wrong. He blows hot and cold, just like the wind. One moment he's happy and excited, and the next he's in the doldrums, dragging his chin on the floor as if he's having to put up with so much hardship in life. I just don't get

In Daddy's Shoes

it. I don't understand," she said, her voice choking on the last word.

"Hey, cheer up. What if I told you that this is fairly normal for ten-year-old boys? I can tell you for a fact that I was that way. I can handle the grumpiness and the sullenness, but I don't like his being rude to you. That's got to stop."

"Yes, I agree. I didn't say anything because I don't understand what's gotten him upset, and I didn't want to make a scene in public."

"That's probably what he's counting on. Why don't you let me talk with him and see if I can get to the bottom of this?"

"Okay, go ahead." She watched as Andy stood and headed for the game room. She hadn't had a chance to tell him about the call from Brandon's grandmother, but the more she thought about it, maybe she shouldn't mention it. The woman was lonely, sad, and possibly bitter. Living without her child was hard on her, and she didn't have any other close relatives living near her and her husband. She probably had high hopes and deep love for Brandon and wished she could see him more often.

The game room door slammed open, the sound jerking her eyes in that direction. Brandon stormed out, his fists at his sides and a determined look in his eyes that said he was furious. Before she could react, he had slammed out the restaurant door.

She whirled her head around to see Andy coming toward her, frowning every bit as much as Brandon when he slid into the booth across from her.

"Well, I guess you can tell the talk didn't go very well." He sighed, picking up his iced tea glass and taking a swallow.

"What did you say to him?"

"I asked him if he realized how rude he had been to you, and he launched like a rocket from NASA. He yelled at me that I wasn't his dad, that I didn't care about him, and that all I wanted was you. When I told him that he was wrong, he slammed out of the room."

Lydia looked out the window of the restaurant and saw Brandon kicking pebbles in the parking lot, his hands shoved deeply into the pockets of his jeans. His head was down, and his lips were a straight line that slashed across his face.

Her heart ached as she watched her hurting son. What could she do to help him? It felt like her back was up against a very hard and cold wall, and the only thing she could do was fight. She'd keep fighting for Brandon until the boy realized how much she cared and how hard she was trying to do what was right for him.

Despite her attempts to draw Brandon out, they left the restaurant and drove home in almost virtual silence. When they arrived at the house, Brandon was out of the truck almost before it came to a stop. He disappeared into the backyard while Lydia helplessly called out, "Brandon?"

"Give him a little time," Andy suggested. "Let him work through his thoughts, and he'll come around. If not, we'll put our heads together again and see what we can come up with. Okay?"

She nodded as a weak smile lifted the edges of her lips. "Thanks for the day. I almost enjoyed it."

He leaned over, lightly touching her lips with his own. "Lydia, I care about both of you more than I can explain, but I see the two of you hurting, and I'm not sure I'm helping by being here." His hand slid under hers, linking with her fingers, feeling hers instantly tighten.

"You may feel that you're the problem at the moment," she told him softly, her right hand coming up to gently touch his cheek while he held her left hand captive, "but you just might be the one thing that can turn him around."

He chuckled ruefully. "Here's hoping," he said. "Heck of a job I'm doing so far, huh?" He nodded toward Brandon.

After stretching the few inches to quickly kiss him, Lydia slid over and opened the door that Brandon had slammed shut, walking around to the driver's side, waiting while the window slid down. Leaning in, she brushed her lips across Andy's one last time. "Thank you for being so patient and for caring about Brandon even when he's acting like this."

"No problem. Call me tonight, and let me know how he's doing. I'll be up late correcting papers," he added, rolling his eyes toward heaven and heaving a sigh. Grading papers was definitely his least favorite thing to do. He much preferred interacting with his high-energy students.

Lydia stepped back and watched him back out of the driveway and leave. A light toot of the horn sounded down the street as he disappeared out of sight.

For the first time in two years, she had hope.

"Hi, Lydia. It's Toby's mother, Helen."

"Oh, hi, Helen." She glanced at the clock. It was ten minutes past eight. "What can I do for you?"

"I was wondering if Toby was over there. I just went in to call him for his shower, and his room is empty. I can't find him."

Lydia's smile vanished when she heard the near panic in

the woman's voice. She could imagine how frightened Helen must be as she waited to hear the answer.

"Helen, Toby isn't here. If you'll hold on a moment, I'll go check with Brandon to see if he might know where Toby is. Hold on," she instructed, laying the phone down. Toby and Brandon were best friends. If Toby was missing . . . Her heart was pounding as she bolted down the hall and shoved open Brandon's bedroom door.

She had left him working on a science project about an hour before, but even before she opened the door to his room, she knew he wouldn't be there.

A cold sweat broke out on her skin as her stomach muscles contracted. "Oh, God," she moaned as she turned and ran to grab the phone.

"Helen, Brandon's gone too," she blurted out.

"Oh, no. This can't be happening." Helen asked the question that both of them were thinking. "Where do you think they could have gone?"

Lydia was pretty sure that her son wasn't at the cemetery again. Why had he left? He had sulked the whole time they were out with Andy, but he had appeared to gradually get over whatever had upset him earlier in the day. He had even volunteered to start on the science project that wasn't due for a few weeks. With the current circumstances, she should have realized that offering to do a project early was a sign that he just wanted her to think he was working in his room while he snuck off.

"Helen, do you have my cell number?"

"Yes, it's on the football squad listing."

"Okay. I'll go out and look for Brandon, and if I find

him or both of them, I'll call you, and you'll let me know if Toby or both of them show up there, agreed?"

"All right. Toby's father is already out looking, but neither of us know where to start." Lydia could hear the tears in the other mother's voice, but she didn't have time to comfort her right now. They didn't even know when the boys had left, so they didn't know how far they might have gone.

As soon as she had said good-bye, she pushed the end button and immediately, instinctively dialed Andy. Fortunately she didn't have long to wait.

"Hello?" The moment she heard his deep voice, she felt a burst of relief. He represented strength, and at the moment she was fresh out of it.

"Andy, it's Lydia. Brandon's gone . . . apparently with Toby," she said, trying not to cry. Andy had once told her that he'd rather face ten hungry lions than one crying female. They had both laughed at the time.

"I'll be over in fifteen minutes. Stay put, and I'll be there as soon as I can, okay?"

"Please hurry," she begged, no longer holding back the tears.

By the time Andy turned into the driveway, Lydia was already out front waiting for him. He had barely come to a stop before she was slipping into the passenger seat.

"Toby's dad is out looking, and they'll call my cell number if they find the boys."

"Do you know if anything happened? Was Brandon still angry?" He backed the truck into the street, jammed it into gear, and left rubber on the pavement when the vehicle leaped forward.

"No, or at least not that I know of. He had been in a somewhat agreeable mood all evening and even volunteered to start on his science project at about seven o'clock," she said, craning her neck to look down each street as they passed. "His bicycle is gone, so no telling how far they've gone."

"That science project isn't due until next month."

"I know."

Quickly looking both ways, he stomped on the gas, shooting through a yellow light just before it turned red.

"Be careful," she cautioned, instinctively reaching out as she would to shield Brandon. "Where are we headed?"

"I thought we'd look at the school, maybe down at the lake. Are there any relatives he might have gone to visit?" Andy slowed the truck as he turned into the school parking lot.

"Steven's parents live about fifty miles or so from here."

"Which way?"

"North up Highway Seventy-five."

"Kids don't always consider distances. They usually don't think too far ahead or reason things out. They just head out toward where they want to go." He pulled into a parking spot, leaving the truck running as he opened the door. He grabbed a flashlight from under the seat before stepping out. "Stay here. I'll check around and be right back."

Lydia watched him jog around the end of the school building, the beam of light bouncing as he jogged. He was heading for the football field. She didn't expect Brandon to be there by himself at night.

Within a couple of minutes she saw Andy coming back. Cold air swirled into the truck as he slid into the cab and turned toward her.

In Daddy's Shoes

"Lydia, we need to call 911."

"What?"

"Don't panic yet. Just listen. I found Brandon's bike leaning against the bleachers. I looked around, and there were tire marks from more than one bike, but only the one bike was there."

Her shaking became violent as the reality of the situation slammed into her. Her teeth chattered as she groped for Andy's hand. "My baby. No, he can't be gone. He . . . he . . ."

"Shh, don't worry yet. We don't know what's happened, and we shouldn't fall apart. Maybe—"

He was interrupted when Lydia's phone rang. She fumbled trying to get it out of her pocket.

"Hello?" Her voice was weak as she clutched the phone to her ear.

"Lydia, this is Helen. Toby just came home. He said that he left Brandon at the school. He was waiting for someone there, and Toby told him he couldn't wait any longer with him or he'd get caught and be in trouble. So, if you go to the school, you'll find him."

"Helen, we're at the school, and Brandon's not here," she said, no longer able to stop the tears now streaming down her face. "His bike is here, but he's not. Helen, I'm so worried."

"Oh, I'm so sorry. Have you called the police?"

"No, we were just getting ready to. Thanks," she said.

"Let me know if I—"

"Helen," Lydia interrupted, "did Toby say who Brandon was waiting for?"

"No, in fact he seemed to slip when he said what little he did, and then he clammed up and wouldn't say another word. I'm almost thinking that he doesn't know who, because Brandon apparently just asked him if he'd ride over there with him because it was getting dark."

"Okay, thanks. If you can get him to tell you anything else, please call me, okay?"

"Absolutely, right away."

"Bye," she said, flipping her phone closed.

"He came over here to meet someone, but she doesn't know who."

She turned her face into Andy's chest and cried.

His hand rubbing her back was comforting, but it didn't solve the problem. They still didn't know where Brandon was.

"We need to call the police. They need to be alerted to watch for him. Do you know what he was wearing?"

"Um, yes, yes, I think so. Jeans and his long-sleeved red sweatshirt."

He dug his phone from his pocket but didn't have time to dial before Lydia's phone rang.

"Hello?" She hated that her voice was shaking, but she couldn't stop the quaver.

"Lydia? This is Jonathan." Lydia had always liked her father-in-law, but she didn't went to talk with him at the moment.

"Hi, Jonathan, listen, I can't talk right now. Can I call you later?"

"Lydia, don't hang up! Are you still there?"

"Yes, but . . ."

"I want you to know that Brandon is here."

"Brandon is there?" She turned to look at Andy. Already he was starting to smile.

In Daddy's Shoes

"Thank the Lord," she heard him murmur.

"Jonathan, how did he get all the way up there?"

"Well, I hate to tell you this, but Brandon called his grandmother, and she went behind my back and got him. I didn't know about it until they showed up here about five minutes ago. I thought she was out shopping. Anyway, I wanted to call because I knew you'd be frantic. You can relax."

"Thank you. Thank you so much. I'm on my way. I'll be there as soon as I can," she said, flipping the phone shut as she dropped her head back on the seat.

"I can't believe that woman," she said aloud. "His grandmother came down here and picked him up and took him home with her." The longer Lydia had to think about it, the angrier she got. "I could have her arrested for kidnapping," she said, looking toward Andy.

"Well, I don't know about that or if you'd be glad you did after you cooled down, but let's get on our way. We have some driving to do before we can get him back home. Buckle up," he warned.

He couldn't believe a grandmother would be party to a child's running away. He couldn't imagine his own grandmother standing behind such foolishness, unless, of course, his safety had been at stake. Of course, if his safety had been at stake, his feisty grandmother would probably have come gunning for the person responsible. For all they knew, Brandon had told fibs, and his grandmother thought he was in danger.

"Does Brandon's grandmother do this sort of thing often?"

"No, but my mother-in-law, she's ... well, she's a bit self-centered. And she still hasn't gotten over the loss of her only son. I think she's critical of how I'm raising Brandon. She called to tell me she's definitely not for his playing football because it's too dangerous a sport."

"What? Does she want him raised in a bubble?"

"Yes." She smiled weakly. "That just might make her happy. On the other hand, she'd probably worry about all the germs inside the bubble. She shared some other negative appraisals as well."

"What?"

"She's not happy about your being on the scene and having so much influence over Brandon."

"But I'm his teacher. What does she expect?" He maneuvered them onto the interstate and increased their speed. She didn't bother to complain, since she, too, wanted to get to Brandon as quickly as possible.

"It wasn't the teacher part that had her concerned. It was the hero worship she heard when she called to talk with Brandon."

"Well, she won't have to listen to that this time. He's probably made me out to be the devil's messenger by now," he quipped, glancing into the rearview mirror before refocusing on the highway ahead of them.

The truck ate up the miles. In less time than she thought possible, yet twice as long as she wanted, they arrived at Jonathan and Marian's home.

The house was ablaze with lights, the Town Car still parked near the front steps.

"Lydia, before we go in there, please let me suggest one thing." When she nodded, he continued. "Please stay calm, regardless of what is said or what is accused. You have the trump card because you're Brandon's mother, and there is

In Daddy's Shoes

nothing they can do to change that and nothing they can do about whom you date. So if they attack you or me, stay calm. If you lose your temper with them or with Brandon, you're playing into her hands. You want to keep Brandon calm, and don't forget, he hates to see you cry, so don't allow them to get to you, okay?"

She nodded as she took a deep breath and opened the door. As long as Andy was beside her, she felt she could face anything.

When she rang the bell, Jonathan opened the door almost immediately.

"Hi, Lydia. Please come in." He extended his hand to Andy when he followed Lydia into the room. "Hi, I'm Jonathan Reynolds. Please come in." He led the way into the living room, where Brandon sat on the sofa, looking at his lap while Marian stood near him, her back straight as a board and her mouth puckered in an expression that screamed her displeasure with the current circumstances.

"Lydia, I'd like to apologize for my wife's being part of this whole affair."

"Don't you apologize for me, Jonathan Reynolds. If you had just stayed out of this, everything would have been fine," Marian objected.

He shook his head in disapproval. "No, my dear. You overstepped your boundaries this evening. You were party to a child running away from his parent because he was unhappy instead of encouraging him to stay and work it out. That's what he needs to learn in order to grow into a responsible adult. How can he do that if he runs away when things get tough? You don't just run away from problems. You face them and work things out."

"Well, look what she's doing to the child," she said, pointing a finger at Brandon. "She's making him be around a man who only wants to be around Lydia. What kind of environment is that for raising a young boy?"

"I'd say it just might be a very healthy one," her husband answered her. Marian sucked in her breath as she frowned at her husband, crossing her arms over her chest.

"It's been two years, and Lydia is a beautiful young woman, and Brandon needs a man in his life." He turned to Andy and Lydia, who were still standing just inside the door. They hadn't said a word but instead had witnessed the first argument Lydia had ever seen the couple have. In the past, Jonathan had always gone along with whatever his wife said, but tonight he evidently felt strongly enough about something to defy his wife's edicts.

"Please, have a seat. Marian, will you get us all some coffee so we can talk about this?"

Andy stepped forward, lowering his voice to talk with Jonathan. "If you don't mind, sir, I would like to have a few minutes alone with Brandon to see if we can work this out."

The older man hesitated for only a moment before he nodded. "Brandon, please come here, son." When the boy stood and walked silently toward his grandfather, Andy watched his eyes dart toward his mother. She smiled reassuringly as she took a seat on the sofa.

"Son, I want you to go with Mr. Jenkins and see if you two can talk this out man-to-man and get it settled. If you need anything, give a yell, and I'll be right here. Okay?" His hand rested gently on the boy's shoulder as he spoke to him. Brandon looked up into his grandfather's eyes and

In Daddy's Shoes 157

then over at Andy before nodding his head and leading the way down the hall toward the bedroom he used when he was visiting overnight.

Andy knew the boy was wrong in thinking that Lydia was the only one important to him, but he wasn't sure the boy would listen to him . . . or believe him.

"Brandon, what if I told you that your mother is sitting out there, scared half to death that her decisions for the two of you have hurt you? What if I told you that she called me this evening, frantic because you were gone?"

"Um," he started, clearing his throat. "Did she cry?"

Andy could barely hear the boy's voice, but he could read his expression. Brandon's head was bowed, his fingers clenched together in his lap as he waited for the answer.

"A little."

"Is she mad at me?" His gaze rose to Andy for a quick moment and then returned to his lap.

"Well, I'm not sure that I'd call it 'mad,' but she's upset, and I think you're going to have to face some form of punishment. Don't you think that's fair when you break the rules?"

"Yeah, I guess," he grumbled. "I'm doomed. I'll be locked up until I'm twenty," he grumbled. "I told Grams and Gramps that my mother wouldn't care that I was gone because she only cared about you."

"Well, I hate to say this, but you don't know your mother very well if you think anyone comes before you in her life. And, for the record, your mother and I care very much about you and your safety. She loves you very much. Brandon, if she had to choose between you and me, I'd lose. In a heartbeat. Do you know that? You are the most important thing to her in this world."

"Then why are you here with her to get me?" His voice had lost the belligerent tone, but he was still frowning.

"When she didn't know where you were, she was scared and called me to help her find you. Remember how I found you the last time?" When he nodded, Andy continued. "Well, I guess she was hoping I'd have as much luck this time. I'm glad she called, because she was too upset to drive carefully."

"Oh." After a few moments, Brandon raised his eyes to stare at his teacher. "Did Toby squeal?"

Andy chuckled before answering. "No, you can trust your friend. He didn't tell, but I'd like to put him on detention for *not* telling. This sort of thing isn't a joke or a game. We were very close to calling the police. The only thing that stopped us was the timing of your grandfather's call. If we had called the police, your grandmother might have gotten into trouble and have had to go before a judge to explain what she did and why."

"They might have arrested her?" His eyes had grown large, and his mouth hung open. It was apparent that Brandon didn't realize that what he had asked of his grandmother and what she had done was illegal. "Why did she do it if she could get into trouble?"

"Because she is your grandparent, and you asked her to. She loves you too."

"I didn't know she could get arrested," he mumbled, obviously rethinking the part he had played in the drama. "Is Mom mad at her?"

In Daddy's Shoes

Andy wanted to be honest with the boy, but he wasn't sure how much to say. "I think you should ask your mother that question. I'm not sure."

"I didn't want anyone to get into trouble, and I didn't want to upset Mom—honest," he said, turning beseeching eyes up to meet Andy's gaze.

"If you didn't want to upset your mother, why did you leave home?"

Brandon remained silent for a few moments, fiddling with a rough fingernail.

"I saw you guys kissing. Toby said if that happened, then it meant that you wanted to spend time with her, not me, and then I got to thinking that I'd just be in the way," he mumbled, his head still lowered.

Andy's heart ached for the boy. He knew how he felt. When his mother dated on occasion, he had always felt in the way, even though his sister had told him that their mother would never choose a man over her two children.

"Brandon, do you remember that I told you about my father's being killed in a car accident?" When the boy nodded, Andy continued. "Well, I used to think the same way you do. But I soon learned that my mother could tell the difference between the guys who only wanted to date her and the ones who cared about her and her family." He waited a few moments for his statement to sink in before he continued.

"And I bet your mother can tell the difference also."

Brandon was now staring up at his teacher, the light of hope in his eyes.

Andy squatted down, bringing his face level with Brandon's.

"I've been meaning to talk with you about your mother, you know."

Brandon scrunched up his face as he stared at his teacher. "What about?"

Andy knew he was running a risk in asking his next question, but he figured the best way to win the war was to enlist Brandon as an ally instead of an enemy. It was worth taking a chance.

"Well, I've been getting to know your mom a little better, and I think I'd like to get to know her *a lot* better, so I wanted to find out if that would be okay with you."

"You're asking me?" Brandon drew his head back and stared at his teacher in total confusion. "I'm just a kid. I'm not even old enough to vote yet."

Andy held in the chuckle that wanted to slip out. This was a serious matter, and he needed to treat it that way. "You're old enough that I would like your permission to date your mother and see if the three of us would make a good team."

A long silence hung between the two. Andy remained quiet, willing to give Brandon as much time as he needed to come to terms with the possibility of a new arrangement. When he was younger, he'd never liked the thought of his mother being with a man other than his dad. How would Brandon feel?

"So you're saying that you want to . . . date my mom? Like take her out to dinner and hold her hand and kiss her and stuff?"

"Yes, that's partially right. I want to date your mother, but most of the time it would be the three of us, not just your mother and I but you also. We'd all go fishing, all go

In Daddy's Shoes

to the movies . . . well, at least most of the time, and both of us would be rooting for you at your games."

As Brandon sat thinking over what had been presented to him, Andy thought of another way to get his point across. "You know how Toby's parents work things out, don't you?" When Brandon shrugged, Andy continued. "Most of the time they do everything as a family, but occasionally Toby has a sleepover at your house so his parents can go out for the evening. Right?"

"Yeah, I guess so."

"Well, this would be a lot like that, except that I'd go home each night. I wouldn't be living with you guys."

"Why not?"

"Because your mother and I aren't married," he said, making sure that he made eye contact with Brandon.

"Don't you want to marry my mom?" Brandon had begun to relax a little as he sat on the edge of the bed.

"Getting married is a big decision that involves both adults wanting the same things and both adults loving each other. I know your mother has some feelings for me, but I don't know if she loves me enough to marry me. But I'm willing to give her time to decide if she loves me enough and wants to have me live in the house as her husband and as your stepfather. In the meantime, we'll have time to get to know each other and have some fun together."

"That's all there is to it?" Brandon looked skeptical, squinting as he quirked his lips up into a pucker.

"I think that's about it, but I'll need your help."

"My help?" Now he was leaning forward slightly, attentive and curious.

"Well, there are two things that upset me, and I need

your help in being sure those two things don't happen. One of them is easy, because I already know you don't like it either."

"What's that?"

"I don't like to see your mother upset or crying." He watched the boy's face change. He knew he had hit a home run on that one. Brandon hated to see his mother cry.

"So what's the other one?"

"I don't like to see anyone be rude to her. I know you know what that means."

"Like talking back to her or yelling—stuff like that?"

"Yeah, stuff like that. Do you think you can work on not doing that?"

There was silence for a few moments while Brandon thought about all that had been said. Andy could see when the boy made up his mind. He raised his head, looked him straight in the eye, and stuck out his hand.

"Yes, and I'll even shake on it," he said seriously.

Andy had trouble keeping his emotions under control. The child was taking a chance on trusting him to be around his mother and was even willing to go the extra mile to help make the relationship work. What more could he ask for?

"Come on, let's go out and rescue your mom." He smiled, using their linked hands to pull Brandon off the bed to stand beside him.

"Uh, I have one more question," the boy announced. He took a moment trying to figure out how to ask the question, but finally he looked at his teacher and blurted out what was on his mind.

"If I misbehave, will you punish me?"

In Daddy's Shoes

"If you do it in the classroom, yes. If you do it at home, that will be up to your mother. However, if you slip up on the agreement that we shook hands on, then you and I will discuss it. That will be just between you and me. Okay?"

"Okay, I guess that works," he said, heading out the door and down the hall toward his mother.

Andy lagged behind to send up a silent prayer that things would remain, at least for the moment, peaceful, and he could take Brandon and Lydia home without the sulking silence that had accompanied them after the movie.

The conversation, what there had been of it, was stilted and cool between Lydia and her mother-in-law. Jonathan stood by the fireplace smoking a pipe, as she had seen him do numerous times before, but he wore a new countenance tonight. For the first time since she had known them, he had stood up to his wife. Lydia couldn't imagine what would be said after they left, but her biggest concern wasn't what would be said between Brandon's grandparents but what was being said between Brandon and Andy right now in the bedroom.

When the bedroom door opened, she jumped to her feet, whirling around to watch Brandon walk down the hallway toward her. She couldn't believe her eyes. He wasn't the same child. There didn't seem to be any anger or resentment. He wasn't smiling, but he had his head up and was walking with purpose. He came to stand in front of her, staring up into her eyes.

"I'm sorry I upset you. Can we go home now?"

Lydia wrapped her arms around her son, rocking him gently as she kissed the top of his head.

"Yes, honey. We can go home."

"That's it? Without even any discussion, you're allowing that man to leave with our grandson?" The older woman was now glaring at her husband, her hands fisted on her hips and her voice loud and demanding.

"Marian, that's enough." Jonathan spoke softly, but his tone was firm.

Lydia watched her mother-in-law's mouth open and shut several times like a fish gulping air. She quickly turned Brandon around and ushered him toward the front door.

"Give us a call soon, and maybe we can all get together for dinner," she called over her shoulder.

"Brandon, you go ahead to the truck, and we'll be right behind you, honey," she said. Andy held the door open for him. As the boy stepped outside, Lydia turned toward the older couple and spoke softly but with conviction.

"You will always be welcome in our home, but don't ever interfere again with how I raise my son. Not ever." She turned and followed Brandon toward the truck.

Andy raised a hand to wave to the older couple standing near the fireplace. "Thanks, Jonathan. For everything," he added before stepping outside and quietly closing the door behind him.

The ride home was quiet, but it wasn't uncomfortable. The radio played popular music and occasionally one of them sang along while the other two moaned and groaned good-naturedly. Soon Brandon dozed off, waking when the truck came to a stop in the driveway near the front steps.

"Come on, buddy, time for bed. Tomorrow is another day," Lydia said, allowing Brandon to lean on her while they walked up the steps.

In Daddy's Shoes 165

The house was quiet after Brandon's bedroom door shut. The two adults stood in the living room, neither speaking, just staring at each other as the stress and emotions of the evening washed over them.

They stepped forward at the same time, his arms wrapping around her while she leaned against his chest. "I was so worried," her muffled voice said against his shirt.

"Shh, I know, I know," he told her, rubbing her back. "He's fine, and I have a feeling that you won't have any more problems with him disappearing."

Lydia drew back, wiping tears from her cheeks as she lifted glistening eyes to meet his. "What makes you think that?"

"Well," he said, his gentle smile beaming down into her upturned face, "we had a man-to-man talk, and I think he understands that I'll be dating his mom, and he didn't seem to have a problem with that."

"Are you sure?" Her heart was thumping as her thoughts wandered to what he had said and what it meant for her future. And Brandon's future. Was she even ready to allow another man into her life?

"Yes, I'm sure. Come over and sit down. I want to tell you a couple of things."

He sat on the sofa, pulling her down to snuggle against his chest. "I think it'll help you to understand Brandon if I share a couple of things that he told me recently."

He had her attention. Even though she feared that he would tell her things that might upset her, she still needed to know. She knew she could handle it.

"He told me that when his dad left for overseas, he said that Brandon was the 'man of the house now.' Then at the funeral people told him the same thing, and the problem is, he doesn't know how to do that."

"Oh, no. I never knew," she said, one hand covering her mouth as her stricken eyes pleaded with Andy to believe her.

"Honey, I know you didn't realize, or you would have taken care of it," he said, squeezing her tighter for a moment. "You see, he knows how to be a ten-year-old boy, playing football and all that, but he doesn't know how to handle the grown-up things." He leaned over to kiss her on the forehead before holding her away at arm's length. "We agreed tonight that I can date you and that we'll see how we work out as a team," he said, smiling down into her eyes.

"As a team?"

"Yeah, a team. We'll do things with Brandon, and occasionally we'll have an adult-type date, and we'll all see how things go. What do you say, 'Mom'? Up to the challenge of dating again?"

It only took a moment for Lydia to make up her mind. "Yes." She beamed, lifting her arms around his neck and leaning in to seal the deal.

Chapter Fifteen

A storm raged outside while the three sat in front of the fireplace and worked on a puzzle. It was almost lunchtime, and Lydia had a pot of chili simmering on the stove, its aroma permeating the house.

"Brandon, have you decided what you're going to be for the Halloween party tonight?"

He glanced up at Andy for a moment before concentrating again on the pieces. He and Andy had a contest going to see who would fit in the most pieces before the chili was ready.

"No, not for sure," he said, trying a piece.

"Well," Lydia said, sitting up for a moment to stretch out her back, "like I told you a few days ago, you could be a pirate, or a clown."

"Jeez, Mom. Those costumes are for little kids. I was Jack Sparrow last year." He tried another piece that didn't fit.

"How about an African big-game hunter?" Andy asked without looking up.

"That won't work," Lydia volunteered. "He can't take a gun, even a plastic one, to school, and what's a game hunter without a rifle?"

"Are you guys trying to distract me?" Brandon sat up, his eyes narrowing with suspicion as he stared at the two. Two pairs of innocent eyes stared back at him before they glanced at each other and burst out laughing.

"I knew it!" Brandon was laughing. He was five pieces ahead and proud of his accomplishment.

"Hey, you have to learn the ways of the world so you won't get duped by the competition when you get older."

"If *I* was doing it, you'd probably say I was cheating," he grumbled, trying another puzzle piece. "Six!"

"Why don't we stop for lunch, and then we can get your costume together for tonight?" Lydia stood, heading for the kitchen.

"So, how about a rock star?" Andy stood, stretching his arms over his head to unkink his back muscles.

"Hey, that would be cool. Maybe you could draw some tattoos on me, and I could use one of Mom's earrings. Hey, Mom, may I use an earring?" His voice carried into the kitchen, drawing her to the connecting door, a wooden spoon in her hand.

"Are you going as a teenage girl or something?"

"Mom," he admonished, rolling his eyes.

"Lunch is ready. Come and get it."

"I win," Brandon declared, jumping to his feet to be first to the dining room table.

Brilliant lights illuminated the school and reflected off puddles of water left over from the rain earlier. When Andy

In Daddy's Shoes

turned into the parking lot, they could hear the music already blasting through the gym doors that were propped open. To enter, everyone had to walk through a makeshift, dimly lit, cobweb-festooned tunnel that twisted and turned before reaching the gym's double doors.

Screams could already be heard as children made their way through. Andy had helped design the tunnel, so he knew about the monsters that popped out and the bats that dropped down in front of your face.

"Cool," Brandon said, listening to a girl's screams.

Lydia had to admit that her son looked pretty cool. With his hair gelled to spike out all over, the fake tattoos, and her gold earring, he looked the part of a young rock star. She hadn't seen him this excited in a long time. She glanced toward Andy, catching his eye as she mouthed, "Thank you." His wink sent a warm glow through her body. Life was smiling on her and her son.

As the evening wore on, Lydia lost track of Brandon. He was somewhere bobbing for apples, throwing darts for prizes, or stuffing himself from the long table of snack food set up along the side wall where the bleachers had been pushed back and draped with black cloth.

Andy had just arrived back from a stroll around the gym.

"Everything all right?" she asked.

"Yeah." He smiled, taking her hand and leaning back against the wall. "The kids are having a ball."

The words were barely out of his mouth when a boy—at least it looked like a boy—came running up.

"Mr. Jenkins, come quick," the child urged. "There's a fight in the boys' bathroom." The child instantly turned and darted away, leaving Andy and Lydia to follow on his heels. Lydia slid to a halt at the bathroom door, figuring it was best if she waited outside. Besides, she knew Andy could take care of whatever was going on inside.

Andy stopped abruptly when he saw Brandon and another boy tussling on the tile floor.

"Stop this fighting immediately!" His voice boomed into the room like the sound of thunder. With two quick strides he had his hands wrapped around the upper arms of both boys, jerking them to their feet and separating them at arm's length.

"He started it!" yelled Brandon, glaring at the other boy as he lunged around the teacher to take another swing at his adversary.

Andy easily kept them apart, squeezing both their arms to get their attention. "Right now I don't care which one of you started it." He turned to the small group of boys gathered to watch the show. "Go back to the party," he told the onlookers. "Move!" His order had the kids scrambling to obey as he turned his attention to the two he still had corralled.

"Now, one at a time, tell me what happened."

"He called me a sissy for wearing an earring, and—"

"I did not, you liar!"

Both boys were still glaring at each other but turned their attention toward the teacher when his voice again bounced off the walls. "Enough!"

"Brandon?" Lydia entered the bathroom, shock enlarging her eyes as she looked at her son.

"It's not my fault, Mom. I didn't start it."

Andy could still feel the defiance in Brandon's stiff shoulders.

In Daddy's Shoes

"Lydia, would you please wait outside?" His voice was low, but the authority in his tone was evident. It was a request, but Lydia knew it wasn't meant as a question. He wasn't really giving her a choice. He expected her to comply.

It took all of her willpower to turn her back on her son and leave him at the mercy of the man who held him by his arm. She knew Andy would be fair with the boys, but she was concerned that Brandon would feel that she was deserting him.

When the three came out a little later, she was relieved to see that the boys were quietly walking side by side, the former anger not evident. Brandon glanced at his mother before heading off toward the games that were in progress.

"Is everything all right?" Lydia knew she sounded anxious, but she was unable to stop herself from asking.

"Yeah, everything is fine. It was just boys being boys," he assured her, dismissing the incident as unimportant.

"Andy, Brandon doesn't get into fights. That's not like him," she argued, her voice raised just enough for him to hear over the noise in the building.

He moved in close, putting his mouth near her ear. "Honey, please let it drop. Brandon was defending himself, and both boys apologized to each other, so I think the best thing is to forget it, okay?" She stood staring up into his eyes, trying to read if he was keeping anything from her, but his face gave nothing away. "Okay?"

"Okay, I guess," she agreed, deciding to defer to his judgment, at least for the moment. It felt strange to have someone else take charge. Did she really want to bring someone into their life who would have the authority to discipline her son without even discussing it with her first? Brandon breaking a school rule was one thing, but what about everyday life? She watched Andy head toward the principal to explain about the disruption to the party.

"Why was Brandon fighting? That's not like him," she mumbled to herself. "I want to know what happened in there, and someone's going to tell me," she muttered, glaring over to where Andy stood talking with the principal.

As the evening wore on, she kept a close eye on her son, but he seemed to be having a good time, even interacting with the boy he had fought with earlier. Her emotions felt tender, bruised, as she thought about how easily Andy seemed to be able to get through to Brandon. She knew it was irrational, but her emotions bounced back and forth between feeling she should be the sole disciplinarian, refusing to relinquish her authority outside of school issues, and then reminding herself that Andy had not only handled Brandon's running away but had handled it with finesse. It rankled that he had been able to defuse a bad situation where she might not have done as well. For all she knew, she might have made it worse.

She was leaning against a wall, shoulders hunched and her hands stuck into the front pockets of her jeans, when Andy walked up laughing.

"Did you see me get the apple?" He held up the fruit like a trophy.

"No, did you bob for it?"

"Nah. A pint-sized witch gave it to me." He chuckled, taking a huge bite.

Lydia found that his amusement was contagious as he

teased her unmercifully about her choice of costume. She had put on an apron and come as a stay-at-home mom. He seemed to be having as much fun as the kids, decked out in black slacks and shirt, his face painted white, and . . . When he got near her, he slipped in his fangs, leaning in to bite her neck.

"Did you come as a vampire just so you'd have an excuse to nibble on my neck?" She giggled as a shiver ran down her arms.

He waggled his dark eyebrows, leering as he growled, "All the better to eat you with."

"You nut, that's the wrong story," she said, playfully slapping at him.

Ten o'clock came sooner than any of the costumed characters wanted, and Lydia and Andy relinquished their chaperone duties and collected the "rock star" to go home and to bed.

The last month had turned cold and had been hectic at work, but Thanksgiving had been a lot of fun, Lydia reflected. Andy's sister, Marisa, had been unable to get off work, but she was scheduled to have three days off over Christmas, and Lydia was eager to get to know her.

She glanced into the rearview mirror at Brandon. Andy had suggested that he write down a few things he wanted for Christmas, so her son was busy working on what appeared to be a very long list. She smiled as she zipped through the intersection near the mall on her way home from the school. The lot was full, and police were directing traffic.

"What's with all the traffic? You'd think everyone was

waiting until the last few weeks to Christmas shop." She grinned, lumping herself in with "everyone." Brandon barely glanced up from his assignment. His list was growing by the minute.

She hummed along to the Christmas music on the radio. She loved music, but she and Steven had long ago sold her piano, since they couldn't keep moving it every time they were assigned to another base.

When she turned the corner, heading down their street, she noticed a large delivery truck parked in front of the house.

"Hey, Brandon, look." She pulled into the drive, leaving the car outside the garage as she stepped out to talk with the man getting out of the truck.

"I'm glad you got home, ma'am. I was about to leave," he remarked, handing her a clipboard to sign.

"What are you delivering?"

"A piano. Merry Christmas." He turned his back and headed for the rear of the truck as another man got out to help.

"A piano?" She turned and looked at Brandon, but he just shrugged.

"Don't ask me. I didn't buy it. My coin bank doesn't hold *that* much."

It had to be from Andy, but how had he known she wanted a piano?

The instrument the men lowered to the street was wrapped in a furniture blanket, effectively hiding it from her view. All she could tell was that it was an upright. Her heart was thumping as she realized that she needed to unlock the front door and figure out where to put it.

In Daddy's Shoes

As the key was turning in the lock, she remembered playing the piano at the school for one of the stage plays that the first and second graders had put on for their teachers and parents. Andy had been there. He must have realized that she played well but didn't have a piano at home and decided to get her one. "That's so sweet," she murmured, "and so extravagant." She was unable to keep a smile from taking over her entire face. Her heart was swollen with love that he had been thoughtful and generous enough to get her such a wonderful, lavish gift.

She hesitated for only a moment to consider how much he had spent and whether or not she should accept it. He obviously wanted her to have it, but not half as much as she wanted to be able to play anytime she wanted again. When she was growing up, she had loved playing, and while her mother was sick, she had played often to entertain and soothe the dying woman.

With their muscles bulging, the two men carried the piano up the front steps and into the living room.

"Where do you want it?"

"I'll move the green chair, and you can put it against that wall over there," she answered, rushing ahead of them to clear the way. "Does your paperwork say who sent it?" she asked.

"No, ma'am, just the name and address where it's to be delivered," he said, unwrapping the furniture blanket while his partner placed the bench seat in front.

She was still mesmerized, staring at the most beautiful gift she had ever received. She couldn't stop the single tear that rolled down her cheek as she lovingly caressed the polished wood.

"Enjoy, and merry Christmas!" With a quick wave, the deliverymen were gone, quietly shutting the front door behind them.

"This is the most fantastic gift," she whispered, running a hand over the spotless wood.

"Wow, this must be your present from Mr. Jenkins. Pretty cool." Brandon had been standing out of the way, but now he sat down on the bench and fiddled with some of the keys, making noise.

"I guess so. I don't know anyone else who would send me such a nice gift." She smiled down at her son. "I guess I'd better fix him a really nice dinner tonight, don't you think?"

As she headed for the kitchen, Brandon followed her. "Hey, Mom, you're not going to make me take piano lessons now, are you?"

She chuckled as the door swung shut behind her. Not a bad idea!

When Andy arrived almost an hour later, he started out denying that he had sent the piano and asking who her new secret admirer was. When she suddenly looked concerned, he burst out laughing.

"Come here. Of course it's from me. I thought you two needed a piano." He pulled her into his arms, wrapping them around her waist and smiling down into her face as she beamed up at him.

"Thank you." She smiled, her eyes closing as she snuggled closer.

"Merry Christmas—a little early," he whispered, leaning in for a long kiss.

In Daddy's Shoes

"Oh, hi, Mr. Jenkins."

Andy had heard the boy coming down the hall but had purposely not pulled away. He wouldn't jump away as if they had been caught doing something they shouldn't have been doing.

"Hi there." He smiled at Brandon as he casually stepped away from Lydia. "Do you think you're up to another slaughter in Roundhouse Five?"

"Yeah!"

"Dinner smells fantastic. How much time do we have?" he asked Lydia.

"I'd say about twenty-five minutes," she said, heading toward the kitchen.

"Well, partner"—he smiled down at Brandon—"I think we've got just about enough time to save the universe, don't you?"

"Yep. I'll be the Duke. Who do you want to be?"

"The Avenger, of course." He grinned wickedly.

"You're on, and may the best man win," Brandon said, sticking out his hand for the older man to shake.

It was just over a week until Christmas, and Andy had offered to take Brandon to the mall. They had been shopping for the past two hours but had little to show for all their efforts. Andy disliked shopping at any time, but he particularly hated fighting the crowds. He would rather be home watching football on his wide-screen television.

Still, he was happy to spend some time helping Brandon shop, and he hoped to have an opportunity to ask Brandon how he'd feel about having him marry his mother.

They wandered into household appliances, and Andy

asked, "Has your mother said anything about wanting anything for the house or the kitchen?"

"No, she said all she needs is more time," Brandon replied, shrugging as he snickered.

"Well, if you see time advertised anywhere, would you please let me know?" He reached over to ruffle Brandon's hair, but the boy ducked, and Andy grabbed him to tickle him. "That'll teach you to get smart with me." He laughed.

Brandon was laughing so hard, he couldn't even protest.

"Actually," Andy said, shepherding them out of the department store and down the mall, slowing to glance into the jewelry store they were passing, "what would you think if I gave your mother something from here for Christmas?" He stopped to look at the earrings, bracelets, and rings glittering behind the glass.

The boy was silent for so long that Andy started to worry. He thought they had been making progress on building a solid relationship, but maybe he was mistaken.

"Brandon?"

"Well, I was wondering what type of jewelry you had in mind," the boy answered, glancing at the various shops, the shoppers, and even Santa and his elves at their station in the mall.

Andy was hoping the boy would look at him, but he looked everywhere else. "Well, never mind," he said. Brandon didn't act as if he wanted Andy to buy his mom jewelry of any kind. And without the boy's agreement, his hopes for a future with Lydia would never work. He decided to drop the subject for the day.

Standing in front of the jewelry store, Brandon didn't know what to say. He couldn't come out and tell Mr. Jenk-

In Daddy's Shoes 179

ins that he wanted him to marry his mom. What if that wasn't what the man had meant? What if he had been thinking about earrings or something?

"Hey, Brandon, how about some lunch?"

"Okay," he answered with forced enthusiasm.

They walked in silence toward the food court at the far end of the mall.

The week before Christmas was busy with shopping and wrapping gifts. On the last day of school before the holidays there was a huge party with several of the parents, including Lydia, making food and arriving at the classrooms to help serve.

Lydia couldn't keep her eyes off Andy as he interacted with his excited students. She knew he would make a great father, if he ever got married again. She had held out hope that he might be thinking about their relationship getting serious—they spent several evenings a week and most weekends together—but Andy had made sure that he kept things on a friendly basis.

"Girlfriend, you're drooling," Helen said, stopping to lean against the wall near Lydia.

"Is it that obvious?" She chuckled as she looked at Toby's mother. They had gotten closer after the boys had performed their disappearing act, each agreeing to keep a watchful eye on the other's son and report anything suspicious. They joked about being tag-team moms.

"Honey, you look like a child staring at the puppies at the pet store. The good thing, though, is that I assume he's already housebroken."

Lydia chose to ignore Helen's reference to Andy, but the

thought wasn't far from her own mind. "You know what? I'm glad you mentioned puppies. I think a pup would make a great gift for Brandon. He's always wanted one."

"You're asking for all kinds of trouble. You know he'll promise to take care of the cute little thing, but within a couple of weeks you'll be the one feeding and picking up behind the precious mutt."

"I hear you, but I think it would be good for Brandon to have the responsibility of taking care of a dog. It'll be great," she said, already making a mental list of the things she would need to get to go along with the dog.

Her friend pushed away from the wall she had been leaning on, rolling her eyes at Lydia. "Good luck!" she tossed over her shoulder as she walked away.

That evening after Brandon went to bed, Lydia called Andy.

He picked up on the first ring. "Hey, beautiful."

Lydia snuggled down farther into her bed as she smiled into the empty room. "Hi. Brandon just went to bed, and I wanted to talk with you about an idea I had."

"Fire away," he encouraged her.

"What do you think about my getting Brandon a puppy for Christmas?" She couldn't wait to hear his answer, wondering if he would agree that her son was old enough to take on the responsibility.

"I think it's a great idea, as long as Brandon's mother remembers that it's Brandon's dog and therefore his job to feed, wash, and most important, pick up behind it. If you're willing to hang tough and insist that he's the owner and therefore the one to do everything, then I think it's a wonderful idea."

In Daddy's Shoes

"I'm so glad you agree. I only wish I'd thought of it sooner. Maybe having a puppy would have helped him this past year."

"Well, if he hadn't had issues, you and I wouldn't be talking right now," he reminded her.

"You have a point there." She laughed softly.

"Lydia, there's something . . ." He cleared his throat before continuing. "I think we need to discuss . . . No, on second thought, I think it should wait until we're together."

Her heart thumped hard in her chest as she clutched the phone to her ear. "Um, can we get together tomorrow?"

"Okay. Oh, wait a minute. I almost forgot that Marisa is coming in tomorrow. Why don't we plan to have dinner? I bet my sister would be happy to come too."

"That would be wonderful. Let's do it here, okay? Talk to you then."

"Good night, honey."

She gently set the phone on the recharging base, sliding down under the covers. She was in love and wished she could tell him, but she hesitated to be the first to make that declaration. Maybe tomorrow night. A smile eased across her face, remaining in place as she drifted off to sleep.

Chapter Sixteen

Christmas was only a few days away, generating a festive mood. School had just gotten out for two weeks, and the kids were filled with candy, cookies, and excitement.

Brandon was waiting in Mr. Jenkins' classroom for a ride home. He could have taken the bus, but his teacher had asked him to wait after school. He couldn't think of anything he had done wrong, but adults were funny sometimes. They'd get all serious when you were kidding or joke when you were serious. He couldn't figure them out.

"Okay," his teacher said, coming through the door and unbuttoning his coat. "Everyone is on the buses, and now we have some time to talk about something very important."

After hanging his coat on a hook near the door, he came to where Brandon was sitting in the front row waiting. Leaning back against his own desk, he cleared his throat before starting.

"Uh, you know that I care a lot about your mother and you, right?" When Brandon nodded, he relaxed a little before continuing. "Well, I've been shopping for a Christmas

In Daddy's Shoes

present for your mother, and I wanted to show it to you first to see what you think," he concluded. He waited for Brandon to say something, and when the boy said, "Sure," he stood up and went back to his coat, pulling something out of the pocket.

When he got back to Brandon, he flipped open a small black box to display a glittering diamond ring nestled in black velvet.

Brandon's eyes widened. Mr. Jenkins wanted to give his mother a diamond ring? His eyes rose to search those of the man standing in front of him.

"So, does this mean that you want to marry my mother? That you're going to ask her to marry you?"

"Well, that all depends. I love you and your mother, but I need to know what you think about my marrying her and moving in to live with you guys."

In Brandon's haste to get out of the chair, it topped over, slamming into one in the next row. He plowed into the big man, wrapping his arms around him and holding on tightly.

"What took you so long? I didn't think you were ever going to ask her! I was beginning to think you didn't want us," he mumbled into Mr. Jenkins' sweater.

Andy's hands plastered the boy to him, holding him while he fought the tears that threatened to fall. His heart pounded as the boy continued to cling to him. Thank goodness Brandon was happy about his Christmas present!

When Brandon pulled back, Andy smiled down into the boy's happy face.

"Well, son, I guess it's up to you and me to convince your mom to marry me. Are you ready?"

A huge smile splashed across Brandon's face, and he nodded. "Ready."

On the way home, Andy called Lydia on his cell phone.

"Hi. Brandon and I thought we'd fix dinner tonight, so if you get home before we do, don't start anything, okay?"

"Wow, now that's an offer I can't refuse. I don't care if it's hot dogs, as long as I don't have to fix them or clean up afterward. You have a deal. See you soon."

"What did she say?" Brandon was excited about the plans they had made. He just hoped his mother would say yes.

"She said we could get away with serving hot dogs, but I think we should stick to our original plan." He smiled across at the boy he hoped would soon be his stepson.

After a stop to buy candles and wine, they went to Antonio's and picked up ready-made lasagna along with salad and garlic bread. The aroma filled the truck, making their stomachs rumble in anticipation.

When they got to the house, they rushed inside to put the casserole into the oven to stay warm, the wine into the refrigerator to stay cool, and to set the table. Marisa was the first to arrive.

"Man, look at this table. Candles and wineglasses. What are we celebrating?" She was taking her coat off as she surveyed the dining room off to her right.

"He's going to—" Brandon began.

"Shh. It's a secret. Now get the matches so we can light the candles before your mother gets here," he instructed.

As Brandon darted toward the kitchen for the matches, Marisa looked into her brother's eyes. She had fretted often that he would never allow himself to love again after his experience with Sheryl, but the glow in his eyes made

In Daddy's Shoes

a slow grin brighten her face, as she nodded, raising her hands to clap, applauding him. "Good job. Good choice."

"Thank you." The words were barely out of his mouth when he heard the garage door open and the car pull in.

"Mom's home!" Brandon said, rushing into the room. Andy could tell how excited the boy was about the evening. He was too, although he was also a little apprehensive. What if she said no? What if he had misread her? He quickly lit the candles, tossing the box of matches into the china hutch drawer.

The door opened, and Lydia breezed in, coming to a sudden stop as she encountered the threesome standing and staring at her.

"Hi." She laughed nervously. "Is everything all right?"

"Oh, yes," Andy said, stepping forward to take her coat and give her a quick kiss.

"So, what's the big occasion?" she asked, glancing at the dining room.

Andy handed her coat to Brandon, who promptly tossed it onto the sofa, his gaze riveted to his mom and Mr. Jenkins.

Lydia looked from one to the other, smiling at Brandon before looking back at Andy. "What's going on?"

It was obvious she was getting a little nervous. Andy had to do something and do it now. "Uh, I wanted to ask you something."

He pulled the jeweler's box from his pocket and stepped forward. Lydia's hand rose to cover her mouth as her eyes grew large, tearing up as she stared at the man standing in front of her.

"Lydia, I've been in love with you for a long time, but I wanted to be sure before I asked you to team up with me.

Will you marry me?" His heart was tap-dancing in his chest as he waited for her reply.

It took several long seconds for her to lower her hand and smile. "Yes. Yes, yes, yes!" Neither knew who moved first, but in one motion they were in each other's arms. When their kiss ended, she leaned back to look into his eyes. "I love you too. I can't believe this."

He opened the box and, taking out the ring, slid it onto the fourth finger of her left hand. "Whew! It's official."

"I was wondering when he'd get up the nerve to ask you," piped up Brandon, all grins.

"Thanks a lot, buddy," Andy said, reaching back to playfully jab Brandon's arm.

"Well, gang, the smells coming from the kitchen are fantastic, and the candles are about to melt all over the table, so I suggest we sit down and eat," Marisa said, ushering the family into the dining room. "I'll bring in the food if you'll help me, Brandon."

When Andy and Lydia were alone, they stole a tender kiss before Andy seated her at the table.

When the food was on the table and everyone was seated, Andy glanced around, noting a few empty chairs that they could work on filling. He held up his glass of wine, and when everyone joined him, he made his toast. "To family."

"Hear, hear!" And Brandon smiled. "Hurray!" he shouted.